MW01075559

Wanted: Shopkeeper

Book 4

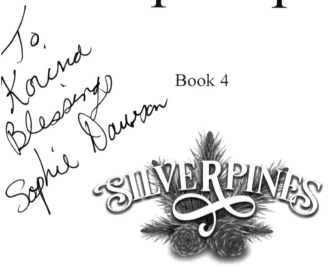

Sophie Dawson

Stories in Faithful Living

Dedication

Wanted: Shopkeeper is dedicated to **Joy Wriston** who lost her battle with cancer on April 18, 2018. She was a sweet person willing to give critique and suggestions to make my novels better. I praise God for her life and look forward to seeing her in heaven.

Silverpines, Oregon
1899

Millie Messer is exhausted and overwhelmed with raising her children and running the mercantile after the death of her husband in the earthquakes that devastated Silverpines. She does what many of the young widows and daughters are doing: Advertise for a Mail Order Husband. She thinks she's found the perfect man to become her helpmate and new father for her four children.

Clay Cutler has a secret, two actually. One will be revealed when he steps off the train in Silverpines. He only hopes Millie doesn't renege on marrying him when she finds out. The other he'll keep to himself until it's necessary to reveal it.

Millie is shocked when not only Clay steps off the train but five children with him. All she wanted was a shopkeeper. Now there are nine children in the family. All she knows is that there are lots of meals to cook and laundry to do. That and the outlaws, conmen, and swindlers who've come to town. Plus, she knows he's keeping something from her.

* * *

Will a new husband and nine children be too much for Millie? Will Clay's secret keep her from trusting him? Will it help protect the town from those who want to cause harm? What mischief can nine children get into? Is Clay the Wanted: Shopkeeper who will heal Millie's broken heart?

CHAPTER ONE

SILVERPINES, OREGON
Late May 1899

Dear Mrs. Messer,

Thank you for responding so quickly to my inquiry. Please, once more, accept my heartfelt sympathy to your loss. I know what you are going through as I lost my beloved Lucy this past January. It is my hope that we can help each other through our grief.

I will reiterate what I told you in my previous letter about myself. I am thirty-four years of age. I have been involved in merchandizing from a very young age as my father owned the general store in Stones Creek, Colorado. Upon his death my siblings and I inherited Cutler's General Store. Enclosed you will find the newspaper clipping detailing this transition. I am standing farthest to the right in the photograph.

You may wonder why I am interested in moving to Oregon when I am established in Stones Creek. The answer is two-fold. The town holds many fond memories as well as family and friends. These include all my memories of Lucy and her loss has dimmed my desire to remain in the community. As the third child of five there is also limited opportunity for growth and advancement within the family business.

If you accept my offer to become your husband I will sell my part of the business here in Stones Creek. I have many years of experience in all aspects of running a mercantile. I believe we could be partners in continuing the success of your business.

There is no need to send funds for travel to Oregon as I have not only savings but will have the proceeds from the sale of my portion of Cutler's General Store.

I have included a letter of reference from Pastor Noah Preston who has known me my entire life. You mentioned in your letter the desire for a faithful Christian husband. I hope this lays any worry you might have on this topic to rest.

I look forward to your reply. I believe I could be in Silverpines within two weeks of receipt of your acceptance of me as your husband to be. With God's help we could aid each other in our grief and I know I can lift the burden you carry of your family and the mercantile.

Awaiting your response.
Sincerely,
Clayton Ryder Cutler

Millie laid the letter on the kitchen table where she was sitting. It was nearly ten o'clock at night, the darkness lit only by the oil lamp she'd carried up from the mercantile she and her family lived above.

She was exhausted. With four children ages from ten-year-old Fern down to eighteen-month-old Abe to tend and the mercantile to run there were simply not enough hours in the day to do all that needed to be done.

Add in her grief at the death of her husband, Sherman, during the terrible events at the time of the earthquakes that hit Silverpines in mid-April and Millie was simply existing, trying to keep up. Each day was harder than the last. Tears of grief and exhaustion came nightly when she finally climbed into her lonely bed unable to face one more of the many tasks that needed to be done.

The devastating earthquakes hadn't taken only Sherman. Both married and single young men had died in the collapse of the Pike Silver Mine with the first quake in April and the mudslide at the Timbertown logging camp the following day after the second. The deaths left many young single women and widows in vulnerable situations and no decent men to give the protection of marriage.

Within days unscrupulous men began arriving in Silverpines trying to swindle the women out of the businesses their husbands and fathers left behind. There were offers for purchase at far below the value of ranches and businesses. Men hired to repair damaged buildings who did shoddy work and expected to be paid premium wages for it. A man who came to town and set up a protection syndicate. These were what caused Millie to attend the meeting at Betsy Sewell's home in mid-May.

At the meeting Betsy had explained how she'd advertised for a husband in the Grooms Gazette, a pamphlet which posted for Mail-Order-Brides. She'd met her new husband, who was also Silverpines' new town marshal through her advertisement. Millie knew she needed help with the store as well as with her children. There simply weren't enough hours in the day to do her chores, tend the children, mind the store, and learn all that was necessary to run the business.

Of all the responses she'd received, the one from Clayton Ryder Cutler had impressed her the most. Rather than ask a lot of questions about the mercantile, he'd expressed his sympathy for her loss and asked how she and the children were coping. He'd told of his willingness to move to Silverpines and help her manage the mercantile.

At the end of his letter of inquiry, Mr. Cutler included a short prayer asking for God's protection over her and her children. Also that she would know whom it was God wanted her to accept as her new husband and helpmate. His letter had shone with the light of the Lord in answer to her prayers for His will.

Millie carefully folded the letter and slipped it back into its envelope. She picked up her fountain pen and put it to paper asking that Mr. Clayton Ryder Cutler move to Silverpines, Oregon and take her as his wife.

Dear Mr. Cutler,

I offer my sympathies for your loss and accept yours for mine. I do hope this letter relieves you somewhat of your grief and helps you look to the future with hope as I am now.

I am pleased to accept your willingness to move to Silverpines and become my husband. I do want to reiterate that I have four children. Fern is ten-years-old and has accepted the burden of caring for her siblings since the death of their father and my needing to work in the mercantile daily. I wish to lift that from her young shoulders. Reuben is eight and very precocious. Opal is four and has been quite despondent since the tragic events. Abe is only eighteen months. It grieves me that he will not remember his father who loved him and the rest of the children so deeply.

Your experience with the family's general store is welcome as I find that, though I often worked alongside my husband, I know little about the management. That as well as the repairs and other issues that have arisen since the disaster have me looking forward to your arrival.

Please send me a telegram as to your arrival. By the first of June the railroad will begin its regular schedule.

Thank you, again, for being willing to make this move and take on me and my children. With God's help we will build a successful marriage honoring both your wife and my husband.

Sincerely yours,
Millie Messer

Clay reread the letter though he knew it by heart. He only hoped Millie had the same optimism when the train arrived in Silverpines. He had told the truth in everything he'd written in the letters he sent her. It was the volume of the omissions that worried him. He had no one to blame but himself if she rejected him on sight. Pastor Noah had warned him he risked everything if he didn't apprise her of his situation before he arrived.

Clay looked up at the ceiling of the railcar. *Lord, you Called me to come. I've always trusted your Callings but none have required this amount of faith. I have so many doubts. You've always been faithful in making each work out and I know You will this time too. Forgive my doubts. Please make the meeting go well. Amen.*

The conductor's call of, "Silverpines, next stop. Silverpines, Oregon in ten minutes," pulled Clay out of his prayer. He looked down as a small hand tapped his knee.

"Pa, that's where we get off, isn't it?" Grace, his five-year-old daughter asked, her eyes shining with excitement and the curiosity always present in her gaze.

"Yes, Pumpkin. It's where we get off and meet the family we will join to ours."

"And I'll have a whole new town to explore." Grace lifted the ever-present magnifying glass to her face, her eye enlarging as the lens was pressed close.

"Yes. Now, help me gather our things. First, go make sure the boys do the same."

"Yes, Pa." Grace ran to the seat behind to relay the message while Clay sent another prayer up that an explosion of TNT wasn't waiting for him at the Silverpines train depot.

CHAPTER TWO

"STAND BESIDE ME, PLEASE." MILLIE held Abe on her hip while Fern stood beside her holding Opal's hand. Reuben bounced on his toes on her other side. They could hear the whistle announcing the arrival of the train that carried the man who would be her new husband.

Millie bit her lip to keep the tears from filling her eyes and overflowing. She missed Sherman so much. She didn't want to marry again, at least not now, but there was no way she could run the mercantile and raise their children.

Each was reacting to the loss of their father in their own way. Even Abe who was only a year and a half was fussier and woke up in the night crying, which he hadn't done since he was a couple months old. All the children were clingy and out of sorts. She was too. Millie was simply exhausted. So much had happened in the past eight weeks.

First, the earthquake which had collapsed the Pike Silver Mine. The following day, the second quake caused further collapse of the mine taking the lives of the men trying to rescue those trapped miners. A massive mudslide of the rain soaked mountainside destroyed nearby Timbertown. Sherman's life ended in the second earthquake while attempting to find anyone still alive in the mine. Its collapse had sealed the fate of any miners trapped as well as the rescuers.

The physical strength needed to run the store had surprised Millie. Lifting, hauling, repairing what she could had taxed her body to its limits. Between the emotional and physical pressures Millie was totally drained.

Fern and Reuben had been good help as the merchandise was either picked up and set to be sold or put in barrels to be disposed of. Even little Opal had spent some time dividing nails by length.

Jackson Hershell, an orphan boy of thirteen came sometimes to help. He did odd jobs around town to earn money. He'd been busy since the earthquake since so many people needed help.

Millie had kept the store closed until the Monday after the earthquakes. She needed the time to begin coming to grips with Sherman's death. The store was a mess with everything shaken off the shelves and mixed together on the floor. The windows on the storefront were cracked. The doorframe twisted a bit so the door scraped the floor as it opened. The glass in the door was cracked. Fortunately most of the windows in the second story hadn't broken.

With the railroad tracks covered in mud no trains could come to town, stopping all commerce to and from Silverpines. What was useable in the store was placed on the shelves. What trash the children couldn't put in barrels Millie simply swept into piles along the walls. There was still a large pile to be sorted in the back room. She didn't have the time to deal with it. There were too many customers needing supplies to repair their buildings or replace household goods.

Millie hadn't known much about the suppliers Sherman ordered from. He had been a competent businessman, successfully building the reputation of Messer Mercantile over the years. She had sent letters to each supplier telling them of the disaster that Silverpines was now and that she would be sending large orders soon. With the railroad now running, orders had been sent. Shipments were arriving. She'd had no clue how she would move them from the railroad warehouse to the store. Clay Cutler arriving today would help with that. At least she hoped he would.

The noise of the train slowing to a stop drowned out all thought. Abe covered his ears and frowned at her. He didn't like loud noises. Millie bounced him slightly, watching the conductor place the step on the platform. She held her breath as the man from the newspaper clipping stepped from the train.

Clay Cutler glanced at her then turned back. He helped a cute little girl off. She had strawberry blonde hair tumbling in messy waves and a broad smile. She looked around with wide curious eyes that took in everything around her. She focused on Millie and her children and the smile widened.

Two boys jumped down and pushed at each other before Mr. Cutler said a sharp word to them. One looked to be about Reuben's age, the other slightly older. They each carried satchels.

Reaching up, the man took a small girl from the arms of a young teenage boy and turned from the train. He looked at Millie and began to slowly cross the platform, holding the toddler and being followed by the other four children.

Millie gritted her teeth trying to keep the neutral expression on her face. He hadn't said anything about having children. And there were five! She nearly collapsed as the weight of the added members to her family crashed onto her shoulders.

"Mrs. Messer, I'm Clayton Cutler. These are my children. This is Ryder who's thirteen. Nathan is eleven. Ben is eight. Grace is five and Ida is two."

Millie must have smiled some sort of welcome as each child came into focus as they were introduced since they smiled back. They were obviously siblings with similar features though their hair varied between strawberry blonde and sandy brown. Eyes of either grey or deep blue studied her or her children somewhat warily. At least the older ones must have had a clue that they were a surprise to her.

"Pleased to meet you... all. I'm Millie Messer. These are my children; Fern who is ten. Reuben is eight. My Opal is four and this is Abe who is a year and a half." She bounced him a little as he looked at the children lined up next to their father.

"Pleased to meet you all," Clay said. "I'll, um, see to our baggage. Come help me, boys." He looked at Ida who he still held and set her down. "Grace, hold your sister's hand. We'll be right back."

Ida's eyes got big and scared as she watched her father and brothers walk away. Ida began to cry. Millie's heart broke. These children had lost their mother and now their home. "Here, Fern, take Abe for me, please. Reuben, you go help with the baggage. Come here, Grace, Ida. It's going to be okay. Your father and brothers will be back in a moment." Millie knelt, gathering the two girls into her arms. Opal came near and patted their backs, adding what comfort she could.

A mound of trunks was growing next to the baggage car. In a very few minutes the door shut, the train blew its whistle, and pulled away from the station.

Clay found the luggage cart and loaded everything onto it. It would be hard to drag along Main Street to Silverpines Inn as the street was dirt and rutted from wagons and horses during rainy times, which was often as the town wasn't all that far up-river from the coast.

Movement from Grace caused Millie to stand. She knew what that squirming was. "Fern, please give Abe back to me. I believe Grace needs the necessary. Please take her into the station." She tipped Grace's face up. "Will you go with her?" The girl nodded, jumping from foot to foot. Ida clutched her sister's hand. "Do you want to go with them?"

Ida nodded and the trio moved to the building. Opal followed behind.

Millie turned, hearing the cart rumble across the platform. Clay's eyes were searching for his daughters. She stepped up to him. "Fern took them to the necessary. They will be back in a moment."

"Is she old enough to handle that responsibility?" He looked at the depot, concern in his gaze.

"Yes, they will be fine." All the boys were examining the tracks so Millie took the opportunity to speak

19

without small ears hearing. Abe, in her arms, didn't count. "You and I need to have a private conversation."

She saw Clay swallow. "Yes, I suppose we do. Please don't be angry."

"We'll see when you give me valid reasons for you to have neglected to mention you had five children. With my four that makes nine. I wanted a husband to ease my burden, not add to it."

"Pa." Grace ran across the platform to him with Ida following close behind.

"We'll go for a walk once the children are settled at the inn. If that is okay with you, that is."

Millie sighed. "I suppose I'll keep the mercantile closed the rest of the day. I need to figure out what to make everyone for dinner and supper. I'm sure your children are hungry."

The three Cutler boys and Reuben bounded up on the last words with large grins on their faces.

Millie was able to open the mercantile for a few hours in the afternoon. Clay had taken everyone to the cafe for dinner, easing her burden to provide a meal on short notice. Now, Fern was monitoring the four youngest napping in the apartment above the store. Reuben was escorting the boys around town, getting into who knew what kind of trouble.

Millie had stayed in the apartment waiting for the young ones to settle to sleep. She took the time to peel and slice potatoes, making two large pans of scalloped potatoes and ham. They would be put in the oven later to be ready to feed everyone for supper. The walk she and Clay would take to speak privately was going to wait until evening.

Clay was wandering around the store, familiarizing himself with what was carried and where it was displayed. The regular organization of the merchandise wasn't evident. Some of the shelves were damaged in the quakes and not yet repaired. Items were just stacked where there was room to place them. There were regularly carried items which weren't available. Stock was low on others. Notes were pinned to empty shelves stating that orders had been placed and to check back to see if they had arrived.

Clay also noted the structural damage to the building. It seemed repairs had been started but not finished or poorly done. He'd see that everything was repaired properly. He'd learned some carpentry from Massot, Stones Creek's crusty builder. Clay wasn't a master builder by any means but he could do what was needed to repair the mercantile. New windows would have to be ordered. All the buildings in town needed them. Many, including this one, had tarps nailed across the openings. It made the room dim and depressing.

The inn he and his family were staying in had served as an infirmary, as had the saloon, after the twin disasters had decimated Silverpines and wiped Timbertown off the map. Rebuilding was slowly happening but with the railroad having been stopped for so long, supplies were slow to get to town. River traffic had been stopped for a while with the mudslide and logjam. It hadn't stopped the conmen from getting to town. Millie had told him of the outlaws who had come and the protection ring that had been set up by Roy Terhall.

It seemed the man had gathered unsavory men who were doing the 'repairs' and outlaws who had been kicked out of their gangs and begun trying to extort money from the vulnerable women left widows or fatherless by the disaster. It was one reason Millie had posted her advertisement.

It might be the reason for his Calling to come to Silverpines. He needed to think and pray about that as well as whether to mention his Callings to Millie. He hoped she didn't think he was a lunatic. In Stones Creek nothing was thought about the Callings. They were understood. Clay wasn't sure if his ancestry would mean anything to the people of Silverpines or not.

The door scraped open and two men entered. They went straight to the counter with the brass National Cash Register on it. Millie was standing nearby and frowned when she saw them. Clay stepped back into the shadows. A tingling went up his spine. These men set off the feelings of his Calling.

"I told you before, Mr. Terhall. I'm not paying you. Marshal Sewell is fully capable of providing the protection to the town and my business," Millie said, eyeing both men.

"Now, Mrs. Messer. I know you heard what happened to the barbershop. I'd hate for that to happen to your business." The man was not overly tall and quite thin. Clay couldn't see his face.

"Shall I take your threats to the marshal?" Millie laid her hands on the counter, leaning forward just a bit.

"And tell him what? It's your word against mine."

"Just leave my store. You aren't interested in

purchasing anything. I could have you arrested for loitering."

Mr. Terhall picked up a tin of tobacco, placing it on the counter. He dug in his vest pocket and put some coins beside it. "There, I've purchased something. Keep the change. Come on, Vern. We have things to do." He tipped his hat and the two men sauntered to the door, casting one last look at Millie.

Clay came out of the shadows and approached the counter. "What happened to the barber shop?"

Millie wiped her hand down her face. "It was broken into by Terhall's men, so it seems. They broke a lot of the furnishings. Some of the businesses have paid what he's wanting. Some of us haven't. I chose not to."

Clay nodded. This wasn't good. Protection racketeers doing damage to back up their threats. Although Terhall hadn't specifically threatened Millie, the implication was there. He would look into this. He didn't want his children to become fodder for a gangster.

Noting Millie's worried frown, Clay changed the focus of their conversation. "I see that there was an attempt at repairing the building damage."

Millie tucked a strand of hair that had come loose behind her ear. "That was supposed to be a competent structural repair. It soon became clear that he either didn't know what he was doing or didn't care. Once the wall was no longer in danger of collapsing, I told him his services were no longer needed. I don't know when the repairs can be redone or who will do them, but at least the building won't fall in on us."

She turned away to place some items on a shelf behind the counter. Her shoulders were slumped and he'd noted her exhaustion. It must have been awful for everyone in the town to go through such a devastating loss. Nearly every man between the ages of about eighteen through fifty had been killed in either the mine collapse or the mudslide.

Widows and daughters were left to pick up the pieces of their lives and continue the businesses that supported them. As the mercantile owner, Millie would have had customers coming constantly to purchase the needed supplies to live and begin repairs to their homes and businesses.

Clay hadn't seen much of the town yet, but what he had seen showed extensive damaged to most structures. A few had collapsed. There was evidence of scavenging the ruins for useable wood.

Guilt began to creep in. Maybe he should have told her about his children. She must see them only as another load on her already burdened shoulders. Then she wouldn't have chosen him to come to Silverpines. He knew this was where he was supposed to be. Knew that his Calling wanted him here. He wasn't sure what all he was supposed to do, but he would start by lifting some of the responsibility off her.

There were things he could do right now as a beginning. He'd examine the half-baked repairs and figure out what he needed to do them correctly. There were piles of trash in the corners. When the boys got back, Ryder and Nate could dispose of them.

Merchandise was haphazardly arranged on the shelves. He figured the items had just been set there rather than in their proper places. That's another thing the boys could do. Even Sherman and Millie's son,

Rueben, could help with that. There was shelving that was too damaged to repair. They'd need to be replaced.

"Millie, I'm going to examine this repair work and see what I need to fix it. Is the lumberyard working?"

"Can you fix it?" A small spark of hope appeared in the back of her eyes. Deep brown eyes that held such fatigue and despair.

"I should be able to. I was taught some carpentry by a man in Stones Creek, Massot. He's a master carpenter. I'm not anywhere close to his skills, but I should be able to do this. When you get windows, the boys and I can install them too. It's time Ryder learned some skills and it won't hurt the other boys to help either."

"That would be wonderful. With the train running now, it shouldn't be long before the windows get here. I've ordered what I need for both floors as well as a new door. There may even be some in the station warehouse now.

"Also, there is probably lumber either in the warehouse or at the lumberyard. Miss Woodson is trying to run the lumberyard. Her father was killed in the mudslide at Timbertown. I helped her learn how to order lumber shipped in."

"I'll figure out what I need and go see her tomorrow."

Running feet could be heard overhead and down the stairs. Soon Opal and Grace ran in from the back room.

"Mama, Fern says Abe stinks. She doesn't want to change him. I helped Ida go potty when she got up. She wants her papa. She's crying again. Can me and Grace have a lemon drop?" Opal held Grace's hand sidling up to the candy jars.

"May Grace and I. Just one each. One mind you,

Opal. No more," Millie said as she went to the door, locking it and turning the framed slate with Closed written in chalk over. The other side had the hours the shop would be open for the day marked on it. "I'm closing the store now. Mr. Cutler, will you please find the boys and make sure they are cleaned up with hands washed when they come to supper?"

Millie swept past him without so much as a glance. Clay watched Grace and Opal get a candy from the jar and pop them in their mouths. They ran by him with smiles and waves. At least one of the Messer females seemed to like him. He didn't think Millie was too fond of him at the moment. Maybe when they spoke in private once the children were settled for the night he could explain why he hadn't told her of his offspring.

CHAPTER THREE

THE OATMEAL BURPED IN THE pot sending up a hot bit that burned slightly when it landed on Millie's hand. She stuck it in her mouth for a moment then wiped her skin with a dishtowel. Bacon was frying. She'd gone down to the ice box in the store and brought up what she hoped would be enough milk.

Her children and the Cutler's would be here in a few minutes for breakfast. Moving the pot to a cooler spot on the stove, she tucked a stray lock of hair behind her ear. The ribbon she'd tied it back with was slipping down its dark length.

Millie looked down at herself. She was going to have breakfast with strangers while she was in her dressing gown. How embarrassing. There just hadn't been time to change into a day dress.

Her night had been spent tossing and turning when she should have been sleeping. Questions, worries, responsibilities, tasks, orders, deliveries, burdens, and threats rolled through her mind whenever she closed her eyes. Over it all was grief.

Millie missed Sherman so. He'd been her rock, her

friend, her lover, the person she loved with all her heart. When he'd left that day to help with the rescue efforts in the mine she'd never thought he wouldn't come back. The shock when the news had been brought had taken Millie to her knees.

The shared grief of so many women and children had pulled the townsfolk left behind together. Most tried to carry on and support one another. Most of the businesses were now being run by wives and daughters of the men who had been killed in the mine collapse or mudslide.

Millie was better prepared than most. She had worked beside Sherman in the mercantile so she knew some about how to proceed. She had to learn about the ordering and deliveries, but at least she knew how to run the cash register and wait on customers.

Many of the women knew nothing of the businesses they were now trying to run. She'd helped several, including Tonya Woodson, the daughter of the lumber mill's owner who died at Timbertown. She was only nineteen and knew absolutely nothing.

Taking two loaves of bread from the bread drawer, Millie began cutting slices. Reuben had run to the bakery yesterday and bought them for her. There was no way she had time to make bread. She needed to get breakfast served, the dishes done, get dressed, and open the mercantile. Oh, she needed to figure something to fix for eleven people for the noon meal. Baked beans and boiled eggs would have to do.

There was always laundry. She'd be so glad when Abe was potty trained. Diapers simply needed to be washed every day. Thank God Ida wasn't in diapers.

Then there was supper. What was she going to fix everyone? She'd send Fern and Reuben to the butcher for ground meat. She could make meatloaf, boiled potatoes, biscuits, green beans. Maybe she'd send one of the Cutler boys to the bakery for a cake for dessert. She didn't have time to make one.

Five more children. Why didn't Mr. Cutler tell her about his family? Well, it didn't take a genius to figure that out. Would she have agreed to his suit if she knew he had five children? Millie hoped he had more than an answer to that question when they finally had a chance to talk.

The plan to speak privately last evening hadn't come to fruition. Ryder, the oldest Cutler, had come with a note shortly before they were supposed to take a walk and discuss the situation. Ida was afraid and didn't want her pa to leave her in a strange room with only her siblings. Millie understood. For a toddler to lose her mother, then move across country to a strange town and stay in a strange place was difficult. She didn't understand and needed the security of her pa being with her when she went to sleep.

But it delayed Millie's and Mr. Cutler's conversation.

And it wouldn't happen until much later in the day. Millie could hear her children in their rooms and many footsteps coming up the staircase on the side of the building. She sighed, picked up her tongs and began moving bacon from the frying pan to the plate already piled high keeping warm in the oven.

When a knock sounded on the door, Opal ran into the kitchen. "I'll let them in, Mama. I can't wait to see Grace again. She's my best friend. I can't wait until she's my sister."

Taking a deep breath and straightening her shoulders, Millie stirred the pot of oatmeal. At least someone was glad there were more children in Silverpines.

Clay surveyed the buildings of the downtown as he headed toward the lumberyard. He could see damage to all and some had collapsed. He could make a living for quite a while just repairing buildings. He'd come to Silverpines to marry Millie and work in her mercantile though.

It was clear that she wasn't happy he hadn't let her know of his children. He didn't blame her. He knew she had four of her own. The pressure of the mercantile, her children, the town's massive losses and her own grief were enough of a burden. She'd advertised for a husband to help her. He'd brought more children whom she must see as only adding to her problems.

His children were, at least to his way of thinking, well behaved, but they were children. Ryder was growing into a responsible young man but he was still only thirteen. He'd be an asset in helping at the store and with his siblings, as long as he didn't disappear as soon as breakfast was over. Clay would make sure Nate and Ben didn't give Millie problems either. They could do some in the store too: sweeping, straightening shelves, stocking. Grace and Ida were just too little to do much.

A man rode toward him, making Clay glance up. The prickle of his Calling had him studying the rider. This man was up to no good. Clay didn't know what his purpose was or how he would achieve it, but he was sure it wasn't for the benefit of others.

Clay's Callings weren't the same as his grandmother's or Great Uncle Nugget Nate Ryder but they helped him with life and helping others when needed. He could tell when someone wasn't genuinely what they said they were. Especially those who were up to no good. He'd helped find some outlaw hideouts back in Colorado and knew a few things were going to happen before they did. Some things would just stand out so he wouldn't overlook them, like the Grooms Gazette he'd noticed at Cutler's General Store.

He'd never looked at it before, just laid them on the shelf with the other periodicals. That day it seemed as if that paper was brighter than the rest. He couldn't not pick it up and read the advertisements. The text of Millie's ad stood out as if it was written in bold letters. That it was a Calling Clay had no doubt. The rest of the day was spent praying for God's direction and clear indication of what Clay should do. That night, after the children were asleep, he'd written the letter that resulted in moving his family to Silverpines.

The man dismounted in front of the saloon and went into the building. Clay walked on past, heading to the lumberyard. The owner and his son were both killed in the disaster. The daughter was trying to run the business. She was only nineteen and knew nothing of the workings of a lumberyard or mill. With Millie's help the girl was learning and not drowning in the work.

Clay entered the lumber mill office. The girl behind the counter looked up from her ledger. She looked as stressed as Millie did. Well, maybe not quite as much. Millie looked exhausted as well as having the weight of the world on her shoulders.

"Good morning, sir. How can I help you?" the young woman asked.

"Good morning. I'm Clay Cutler and I have a list of items I need to fix the mercantile. Mrs. Messer said you had some window glass and lumber already ordered for her."

"Yes, I'll need to show you which glass panes they are and where the lumber is. I'm sorry I can't carry them for you or have them delivered. You'll have to arrange for that yourself. Oh, I'm Miss Woodson."

"Pleased to meet you, Miss Woodson. I'm sorry for your loss." Clay held out a hand for her to shake as she came around the counter.

It didn't take long for Clay to pile the lumber he needed into a stack. He leaned the panes against it, then went back to the hotel to get Ryder and Nate. They'd help load a push cart to transport it all to the mercantile. It was time both boys learned a thing or two about carpentry. He also needed some hands to hold boards in place and help measure. Besides, it would keep them out of trouble and Millie's hair.

The morning went better than Millie had hoped. Fern, Opal, Grace, and Ida stayed upstairs to play and mind Abe. Clay enlisted the boys to help him. Ryder and Nate, his older two, with the repairs to the building.

Reuben and Ben were set to sorting the pile of goods damaged by the earthquake but not totally useless. All Millie had done at the time was dispose of those that obviously couldn't be sold and put the rest in a corner of the back room. Damaged stock could be sold at a discount or given to people in need.

With Clay at the mercantile it was possible for her to do some laundry and other chores that had to be done upstairs. While she was in the apartment it occurred to Millie that the space allotted wouldn't fit six more people. Besides the living area, kitchen, and bedrooms there was space used for storage of inventory for the mercantile. Some of it would have to be converted into bedrooms.

That thought stopped Millie cold. Was she truly assuming she was still going to marry Clay Cutler? She wiped her hand down her face. She'd wanted, needed, a husband to help her with the mercantile. Her children needed a father. If she didn't marry Clay she'd have to start the process all over. Clay's letter stood out from all the others she'd received. The rest seemed to be bragging about their capabilities or asked how prosperous the mercantile was. Clay was the only man who expressed sympathy for her loss.

Taking time to have a cup of coffee, Millie sat at the kitchen table. She could hear the children in the parlor. The girls were getting along. The giggles made her smile. Fern and Opal hadn't laughed much since their father died. Abe was beginning to return to his normal happiness. He'd asked for Papa for several weeks but had stopped.

The toddler came in and patted her arm. "Hungee,

Mama."

Millie leaned over, kissing him on the head. "How about some bread and butter? I'll make some for you and the girls."

"Gace, Ida too?"

She smiled. "Yes, Grace and Ida too. Go tell them."

Abe ran off to deliver his message. Millie buttered several slices of bread, setting them on napkins on the table.

As she watched the children eat their snack, Millie decided that if Clay was able to explain his reasons for not letting her know about his family, she'd marry him. But she'd make him stew a bit before she let him know her decision.

Clay walked beside Millie toward the river. She had fixed a simple noon meal for them all. They'd closed the store for the day. He'd set Ryder and Nate to washing the dishes. The youngest four children were napping with Fern minding them. Ben and Reuben were still sorting the pile of mixed stock in the back room. Now was the time for the adults to have their private discussion.

Clay ran a finger around his collar. It seemed to be getting tighter with each step. He knew why he'd come and why he hadn't told her about the children. Would she believe him or tell him to leave Silverpines? Glancing up at the sky, Clay said a silent prayer asking for the right words to convince her it was God's plan that they marry.

The day was warm and sunny. A light breeze kept the insects from pestering them. The river glistened as the water flowed past the town. A blue heron stood in the shallows waiting amongst the reeds for a small fish or frog. There were broken logs along the opposite shore as well as on the shore of an island just upstream from town, a reminder of the calamity that had happened nearly two months ago. A bench was on a small dock with a rowboat tied to it. Clay wiped it off with his handkerchief before Millie sat down. He sat beside her.

"This is a beautiful spot," Clay said.

"Yes, other than the logs. I hope they drift away or are pulled from the river. It's not a pleasant reminder."

"No, I suppose not."

They were silent for several minutes. Clay wondered how to bring up the topic they needed to discuss. He was at fault for the issue at hand. It was up to him to begin the conversation.

"Mrs. Messer, I regret not informing you of the extent of my family. I know it was a shock to find out I had five children. It will take me a bit to explain. Please know that I didn't want to deceive you. I know it was God's plan that we come to Silverpines and blend our families.

"I prayed and trusted that His directions leading me here were clear. I didn't trust that He would direct your way to accept me and my children if I told you about them. I was wrong.

"I live by Proverbs 3:5-6. *Trust in the Lord with all your heart and lean not on your own understanding. In all your ways acknowledge him, And he will direct your paths.* My lack of faith and trust has caused you stress and worry. Please, accept my apology."

Millie looked at him, searching his eyes for a long time. Finally, she took a deep breath and let it out slowly. "I accept your apology. I forgive you. I'm still somewhat in shock that if we marry I will become the mother of nine children. Nine. On top of the burden I'm loaded with now, it seems overwhelming."

"I understand. I saw it in your eyes when we walked across the station platform. You hid it well from the children, but I was well aware of it. Maybe because I knew of the shock I was delivering to you."

Millie looked out over the river. Her profile reflected the beauty of her face. Clay knew her eyes were a deep chestnut brown, warm and alluring. They were shaded by her straw hat, pinned into the swirls of her hairdo. He couldn't decide if the locks were dark brown or black. He tightened his hands into fists to keep them from reaching into the waves to see how soft they were.

"Mrs. Messer, I promise to do all I can to take on as many of your responsibilities as possible. I know merchandising. Ryder is good help and has learned quite a lot for his age. I plan to train all the boys, mine and yours, too. Reuben seems to be a good worker."

Millie looked at him with a soft, sad smile. "He and Fern have learned a lot in the past couple of months."

"My boys have too, since January." There really wasn't anything to add. Both knew the reasons.

Her continued silence as they sat watching the river worried him. Millie hadn't said whether she was still willing to marry him. She stared across the river at the far shore.

Clay didn't know what he'd do if they didn't marry. He'd sold his portion of Cutler's General Store in Stones Creek, Colorado to his siblings. Uprooted his children as they grieved for their mother, moving them from everything and everyone familiar. Because he hadn't trusted the Calling of the Lord he'd made a crucial mistake in not telling Millie Messer of his offspring.

Waiting, Clay rubbed his hands on his trousers. His palms were damp. Nervous sweat beaded on his forehead, causing him to wipe his brow with his handkerchief.

There was nothing more he could say. It was all up to her. She would decide if his lack of truthfulness ended their relationship before it started.

Long moments later, Millie turned to face him. The look on her face wasn't encouraging. Clay's heart clenched.

"Mr. Cutler, I will say I was distressed at the thought of taking on five more children. I have barely been able to manage the mercantile and my family. Fern and Reuben have been a great help but still, I've been overwhelmed with everything.

"I, too, try to live by Proverbs three: five and six. It's been so very difficult the last two months. I truly appreciate your confession and acceptance of your error. Many people will not do so. That you did shows your character."

Millie paused and looked out over the river again. She turned back to look at him.

"One thing about our Lord, when we step off the path He wants us to tread, He allows us to. We are always free to choose His way or our own. The most wonderful thing is that when we want to step back into the path of His will, God is always there, welcoming us to continue our journey with Him.

"I believe that God has a plan for you, me, and our

children. I believe that plan is for us to travel with Him together. If we trust in and acknowledge Him, He will direct our path.

"Mr. Cutler, I will honor our plan to marry which we set out in our letters."

Clay let out the breath he hadn't realized he was holding. "Thank you, Mrs. Messer. I believe as you do. That God planned for us to be together." He took her hand in his and brought it to his lips, kissing it softly. "We need to begin making plans. When do you want to have the ceremony?"

CHAPTER FOUR

CLAY AND MILLIE WENT BACK to the mercantile. They'd decided to marry on Monday. That would give them several days to make adjustments to the upper story of the building. Tomorrow they would see Pastor James to arrange for the ceremony. At the moment they needed to let the children know and Clay needed to see the apartment as well as the storage space to plan for the additional rooms.

When they entered the mercantile Ryder and Nate had a bucket of soapy water and were wiping down the shelves. Millie's eyes widened and her mouth dropped open. Clay looked at her and chuckled.

"I see you are surprised. This was a chore they had to do each week at the general store back in Stones Creek. Their cousins all had chores too. It starts when they reach age ten. By the time they are grown they'll know all about running a general store. It's how we all learned." He stepped further into the room. "Good job, boys. I'm proud you took it upon yourselves to do this. I appreciate your forethought and initiative. I'm sure Mrs. Messer does too."

"I most certainly do. Cleaning the store has fallen off the list of tasks that needed to be done the past couple of months." She smiled broadly at them. "Right now, please finish with those you are working on and replace the stock please. Then come upstairs." She held up a parcel. "I've got cookies."

Clay turned the sign to closed and locked the door. They entered the back room and found Reuben and Ben building with alphabet blocks that had been in the pile of unsorted goods. A quick survey showed progress had been made in the sorting so nothing was mentioned of the detour from their appointed task.

"Clean up your blocks, boys. Come up when you're done," Clay instructed.

"I've got cookies," Millie coaxed with a smile. Two eight-year-olds hurried to shove the blocks into a corner.

Millie left Clay in the parlor with Fern, Opal, Grace and Ida, going into her bedroom to remove her hat. As she came down the hall a sound like a herd of stampeding horses came up the stairs. Peeking into the boys' bedroom she saw that Abe was still sound asleep. She went into the kitchen, getting a pitcher of milk from the ice box and a stack of napkins. "Fern," she called. "Will you please help me get glasses?"

Fern's as well as other girls' voices said they'd help. Soon everyone but Abe was sitting around the table in the dining room. Fortunately, they had put all the leaves in the day before. The chairs were mismatched as there weren't ten matching chairs in the apartment. Cookies and milk were being consumed at a fast pace, crumbs scattering across the table and floor.

Clay sat at one end with Millie next to him.

"Children, you know," he began, "that we Cutlers came to Silverpines for me to marry Mrs. Messer. At least that was the hope."

Millie watched the children. Doubt, fear, hope, and uncertainty stood out on all the faces. She was glad they were not going to disappoint those she loved or the Cutlers.

"You'll be pleased to know that we have discussed the matter and on Monday we are marrying. Until then, we, my children and me, will be staying at the inn. Then we'll move in here and become one family."

There were expressions of delight and one comment.

"One big family," Ben Cutler said.

Millie heard Abe calling from his crib. She went to get him. When they returned she saw a quizzical look on Opal's face. She set Abe in his highchair and gave him a cookie. "What is it, sweetie?"

Opal turned her puzzled face to her. "Mama, where's everyone going to sleep? We don't have enough beds. Fern and me already sleep in the bed in our room."

"Fern and I. That hasn't been figured out yet. Mr. Cutler and I will be discussing that."

"Don't worry, no one will have to sleep on the floor. Well, maybe some at first until we get the beds we need," Clay said.

Grace, sitting next to her father tapped his arm.

"Yes, Grace?"

"Pa, what are we going to call Mrs. Messer and what are the others going to call you?"

Millie and Clay looked at each other. That was something they hadn't considered. Some blended families called the step-parent by their surname. Millie didn't want to be called Mrs. Cutler by her new children but wasn't sure what else was appropriate or what the alternative might be.

Nate, Clay's eleven-year-old raised a tentative hand.

"Yes, son," Clay said.

"Um, I've noticed something. Maybe it would help."

All eyes turned to him. His face blushed bright red. He swallowed. "We," he indicated his siblings, "Call you Pa and called Ma, Ma. They," he pointed to the Messer children. "Call their mother 'Mama.' I figure they called their pa Papa. My Ma will always be my Ma. I'd call Mrs. Messer 'Mama.' I'm thinking they could call you Pa."

Millie could tell all the children but Abe were thinking. She looked at Clay. He seemed to communicate silently that whatever the children decided would be okay with him. She gave a slight nod.

Fern was the first to speak up. "I'm fine with Pa. I can remember my Papa but have a pa."

There was general agreement to Nate's plan. Ryder frowned a bit. Millie wondered if he didn't like the idea or was peeved that he hadn't thought of it himself.

"When can we start calling you Pa?" Opal asked. Her eyes were twinkling with delight. Millie was relieved that her younger daughter was accepting of all the changes that were occurring. She'd taken the death of her father hard. She hadn't been enthusiastic about Millie writing to find a new husband and father. It seemed that having Grace and Ida to play with tipped the scales in favor of the marriage.

"Although it won't be official until Monday, I don't suppose it will hurt to start now. If it's alright with Mrs.

Messer," Clay said.

"It's Mama, not Mrs. Messer," Grace said, smiling broadly.

Millie was pleased that everyone seemed to be enthusiastic about the marriage and the influx of siblings. She prayed the camaraderie would continue but knew it wouldn't. There would be adjustments, fights, tears, and hurtful words. Such was the way of children.

Since the day was sunny, they sent the children out to play in the park across the street from the mercantile. Neither Clay or Millie wanted input from any of them while they discussed the needs of the apartment.

Clay let Millie show him around. Then he paced each room as well as the storage area. That was a mess. Obviously nothing had been done in there since the earthquake. Crates were scattered and broken, their contents spilled. He asked for some paper and a pencil and, at the dining room table, drew a rough sketch. Tapping the pencil on the table, he considered how to adjust the space and put in the improvements he wanted to make.

Millie was in the kitchen preparing supper. She came in with a glass of ice tea. "I thought you might like a drink."

"Thank you." Clay smiled up at her. She was lovely. Kind and forgiving. A surge of desire surprised him. They hadn't spoken of the physical side of the marriage. It was something they would have to address. Before the wedding. He wanted to know what her expectations were. He figured she would want to wait to totally fulfill the vows. He did too. It was too soon after Lucy died. Or at least he thought it was. His body was saying something different.

"How're the plans for the apartment coming? Is it going to be difficult to add a bedroom?" She sat next to him, studying the drawings he'd made.

"Not really. We can use the existing door from the apartment to the storage room and add two bedrooms there. One for the older boys and one for Fern. The girls' bedroom now simply isn't large enough for four girls. It would take another double bed or two single ones. We'll also build a room for the boys here." Clay pointed out where the new bedrooms would go.

"What about Abe? He can't be in with the older boys. They'd keep him awake."

"I know. This is what's going to be more complicated since I want to add a room with a bathtub, lavatory, and laundry sinks."

"What?"

"We can't have eleven people trying to bathe in the kitchen. You and the girls need more privacy than that. Besides, trying to get everyone bathed as well as meals fixed just won't work. I like to eat too much to have my food be that late."

Millie chuckled. "So, how are you going to fit that in?"

"Here. We can move the linen closet across from the new bedrooms. Maybe even make it larger. Then cut the existing boys room in half for Abe. He'll move in with the other boys when he gets older. The bathroom fits then." Clay decided to broach the other issue on his mind, or in his body. "That will leave the small bedroom for a nursery in the event of another child later."

Millie looked at him in horror. "Another child? We already have nine."

Clay lifted an eyebrow. He didn't say anything else, just looked at her. Realization dawned on her face. A bright red blush flashed up her neck to her forehead.

Millie glanced back down at the drawing. "Later. Much later. I'm not sure I can deal with the prospect of more children at the moment."

Clay cleared his throat, moving the conversation back to the remodel. "We can build the bedrooms first. Those are most important. Not very difficult either. The boys can help. I thought to put bunkbeds in the boys' room. They can pretend they are cowboys."

Millie laughed. She tapped the drawing. "So where are they going to sleep while the rooms are being built?"

"We'll clear a space in the storage room for the boys. They can sleep on the floor. Fern will have to stay with the little girls until I get hers built. It'll be crowded but temporary. Hers will be first. Then the boys', then dividing for the bathroom and Abe's. The bathroom will be last. At least the fixtures and plumbing. I can tap off the water line in the kitchen to take water to the bathroom. I'll put a stove and water tank for hot water in there too."

"You are one talented gent. Or at least you claim to be. We'll see how this whole thing comes together." Millie's teasing smile brought a tightening to Clay's chest.

After supper Millie and Clay kept the children at the table. They needed to let them know about how the apartment would be changed.

"Reuben and Abe's room is going to be made smaller so we can put in a bathing room," Clay began.

"With a real bathtub?" Grace asked.

"Yes, a real bathtub. Abe will stay in his small room. I'll build a room for the older boys. You'll have to sleep on the floor in the storage room until it's done. Grace and Ida will share with Fern and Opal."

Fern jumped up, knocking her chair over. She ran down the hall, slamming the door of her bedroom closed.

Millie looked at Clay. She got up and went to see what was wrong with her daughter. Millie stopped as she approached the end of the hall. She took a deep breath. She was so tired. So very weary. The decision to marry Clay had lifted some of the burden on her but it came rushing back with Fern's distress. What was the matter?

Knocking on the door, Millie heard sobs. She opened it slowly and saw her oldest child lying on her stomach weeping into her pillow. Sitting down next to Fern she began rubbing her back.

"What's the matter, Dolly?" Millie realized she hadn't called Fern the pet name since the earthquake. Sherman started calling her Dolly when she was a tiny baby. The thought brought tears to her eyes.

"The boys get a new room and don't have to share with the baby. I'm stuck with the little girls. I have to take care of Opal and Abe all the time now. I never get to play with Betty anymore." Fern sobbed again.

Millie realized how much she'd placed on Fern's ten-year-old shoulders. Since Sherman died and she'd been so swamped, Fern became the one who took care of the little ones. It was one of the reasons Millie had placed the ad in the Grooms Gazette.

"You've been so wonderful all this time. I'm so proud of how you've helped me. You've been an angel and," Millie leaned down hugging her daughter. "You left before Mr. Cutler could tell you about the rest of the plans. There's something I think will make you very happy. Come hear what his plan is."

Fern turned over. "Something for me?"

"Yes. Now, wipe your face and come."

Clay was giving instructions to the boys about their chores to help with the remodel when they arrived in the dining room. "Come here, Fern," he said, holding out his arm so she could come close. "Look here." He pointed to a square on the drawing. "What's that say?"

Fern leaned down to look. A smile broke out on her face. "Fern's room. You mean I get a room all to myself?" She looked from her mother to Clay.

"Yes, Dolly. The room you share with Opal is too small for all four of you. There will be a room made just for you." Millie placed a hand on her shoulder.

"Yours will be the first room made since you four girls will have to share until it's done. We can't have you sleeping on the floor with the boys." Clay ruffled her hair.

"Thank you, Mama." She hugged Millie then turned and hugged Clay. "Thank you, Pa."

Bittersweet tears rose in Millie eyes. She was delighted Fern was happy about the room but sad that it wasn't Sherman who was giving it to her.

Sophie Dawson

CHAPTER FIVE

MILLIE AND CLAY FOLLOWED THEIR brood along the park toward the inn. They were going to have a celebratory lunch there. The children were dressed in their Sunday go-to-meeting clothes, all spit polished. They were coming from the church where the marriage ceremony had been held. Millie was now Mrs. Cutler. Clay had placed a wide gold band on her finger. She'd removed her ring from Sherman last night, placing it in a small porcelain box he'd given her last Christmas.

The ceremony had been simple, as had most of the ones performed recently. Pastor James, the new preacher, officiated with his new wife Abby, and Mrs. Fannie Pearl Edmonson, the widow of the old preacher, as witnesses.

Mrs. Edmonson was joining the new family for their meal. She was a spitfire of an older woman and knew her Bible backwards and forwards. Beloved of most of the townsfolk but not very popular with those who frequented or worked at the Lucky Lady Saloon.

She walked between Opal and Grace, the latter inspecting her wrinkled, spotted hand with her magnifying glass. Grace took it everywhere, stowing it in her pocket. Ida held Opal's hand.

The past few days had been a whirlwind of activity. Trunks were moved from the inn to the storage room which was cleaned and rearranged. Clay ordered the lumber needed for the rooms he was to build and worked hard on getting all the repairs done to the building.

Ryder helped with those and worked as a clerk helping customers. Millie was impressed with his knowledge and at how hard he worked. Nate was given the task of fetching and carrying for his father. Reuben and Ben kept sorting and arranging the items in the pile in the back room. It was slowly getting smaller. Millie had a feeling quite a bit of the time was spent playing with the blocks.

Fern was still in charge of the little girls and Abe. With the promise of her own room her attitude improved. The girls seemed to be forging close bonds. Abe was content to simply play with whatever they let him. Millie hoped that she could return to being primarily a mother once the repairs and remodeling were complete. Fern needed to have time for herself and to play with her friends.

In the inn dining room several tables had to be pushed together. Clay ordered the special for everyone. That was much easier for all concerned with this large a group of mainly children. He'd placed an order for a cake for dessert the other day.

A throat cleared behind Clay and Millie and Mr. Terhall stepped up to the table. "Good day, Mrs. Messer. What a fine group of youngsters you have here. I haven't seen many of these before. Are they relatives of yours?"

Clay pushed back his chair and stood. He held out his hand. "Clay Cutler. These are my children. Mrs. Messer is now Mrs. Cutler." The squeeze he gave to Terhall's gloved hand as they shook conveyed the message that he wasn't someone to take advantage of.

"Ah, welcome to Silverpines, Mr. Cutler. I'm sure we'll be mighty fine neighbors."

Clay inclined his head, not wanting to give an affirmative answer. "I'll be seeing you when you come to the mercantile, I'm sure. Also at church." Clay knew he was baiting the man.

"Possibly, possibly." Terhall focused on Millie. "Congratulations, Mrs. Cutler. My best wishes on your marriage. Until next time we meet." He tipped his hat to Millie and Mrs. Edmonson and turned his back to walk away.

"Pa, that man's mean," Ryder whispered. He sat next to his father.

"I know. We'll talk about it later," was Clay's soft reply, patting his son's shoulder. He was beginning to show signs of having the Calling. He didn't want to have a discussion about it now. He hadn't mentioned the Callings to Millie. He didn't know how she would react. That topic was best revealed in private.

Millie checked on Abe who was sleeping alone in the room he'd shared with Reuben. The rest of the boys were in a cleared area in the storage room on pallets. They were excited about sleeping on the floor. They were pretending to be cowboys out on the range. They had even piled some wood scraps into a pretend fire. Millie wondered how long the wood floor would be such an exciting bed.

Reuben's bed had been moved into the girls' room for Fern. The other three would share the double bed. She could hear giggling as she approached the closed door.

Millie smiled. Between the 'cowboys' in the storage room and giggling girls in the bedroom she wondered how much sleeping would take place tonight. She decided to give one warning to each group then simply let it all slide. The newness would wear off in a few days.

After saying a final goodnight to both groups, Millie went back to the parlor. Clay was reading the newspaper. Her stomach was filled with butterflies. Thousands of them. Tonight she would sleep next to a man she knew very little about. She knew details and believed he was honorable, but it felt wrong to be in bed with a man who wasn't Sherman. Was he feeling the same? Was he thinking about his late wife as he hid behind the paper?

It was strange but that thought eased her nervousness. He had to still be grieving for Lucy. This would be an awkward night for both of them.

Millie went into the kitchen, planning her meals for the next day in her head. Several of the children liked ready-to-eat cereals, Wheatena or Shredded Wheat. Others liked eggs or oatmeal. The box of Quaker Oats was nearly empty. She would get a new one from the mercantile tomorrow.

Details of the changes that would have to be made to accommodate six more stomachs to fill ran through her head. More milk, eggs, flour, meat, vegetables. Maybe they needed a larger or second icebox. The dining table was large enough with its leaves. Maybe someday they could get all matching chairs. Other, more pressing needs made that a dream for the future.

Millie wound the clock that sat on a shelf by the window. Taking her lantern she went back into the parlor. "Um, C-Clay." His first name didn't roll off her tongue gracefully.

The newspaper dropped into his lap as his arms lowered suddenly.

"I'm going to retire now." Millie stopped. She didn't know what else to say. He would be joining her soon. She just hoped he'd give her time to change into her nightgown before he did.

She heard Clay clear his throat. "Okay. I'll be in — um, as soon as I finish the paper." The newspaper rose and covered his face again. Seems he was as nervous as she was.

Millie set the lantern on the small table beside the bed, Sherman's side. Her heart ached and she fought down the tears that threatened. Changing into her nightgown, she braided her hair as quickly as she could. When she heard footsteps approaching, Millie jumped into bed, pulling the covers up to her chin. She closed her eyes tightly, trying to block out the light.

Clay entered. Shoes were placed on the floor by the door. She could hear his clothes rustling. The bed sagged as he sat down. Millie held her breath. Covers lifted and he slid in beside her.

Silence reigned.

He shifted. The lantern wick was lowered and the light went out.

Millie held her breath. Would he turn to her expecting anything?

"Goodnight, Millie." His voice was soft in the darkness. He turned onto his side away from her.

Releasing her breath she replied, "Goodnight, Clay.

"I'm going to meet with Marshal Sewell this morning. I want to learn what I can about this Terhall fellow," Clay said at breakfast. He took a sip of his coffee.

"Can I come?" Ryder asked.

Clay knew his son wanted to talk with him about his feelings about the man. Ryder had been warned not to mention the Callings, as had Nate. Both boys knew of the family trait and had for several years. Ben was told to hold his tongue too. Ryder was beginning to experience it. Time would tell if any of his other children were so blessed.

"Not this time, son. You've got responsibilities this morning in the mercantile. Help with clerking and chalk the glass we replaced in the windows the other day. This afternoon we'll begin on that door."

Ryder was disappointed but said, "Yes, sir."

With the boys assigned their tasks, Clay went to the jail. Marshal Sewell was there. The man was tall and lean with neatly trimmed wavy black hair. His blue-gray eyes told Clay he was smart and tough. This man knew what he was doing. He wasn't a man you wanted to be on the wrong side of.

"Morning. How can I help you, Mr. Cutler?" Marshal Sewell laid the pen he was writing with on the desk and stood. The two men had met at church on Sunday.

Clay held out his hand and Marshal Sewell took it in a firm grip. "Please, call me Clay. I'd like to discuss some of the goings on in town."

"Oh? Have a seat. Would you like some coffee? Call me Alex. I'm not much for titles."

"Thank you."

When they had steaming cups in their hands Clay said, "I've just married Millie Messer. You understand the dynamics, I'm sure. There are several other men who've come to town in the same way."

"Yes. I'm one. My wife Betsy is the one who told the other women how she placed an advertisement. That was back before the earthquake. We married in February."

"So you know of the problems some of the women and businesses have been having." Clay sipped his coffee.

"Yes, there've been conmen and outlaws. I've taken out a few but can't get a handle on some of them."

"Roy Terhall one of these conmen?"

"Yeah, he's one. I know he's running a protection racket but can't get enough evidence to arrest him. You had dealings with him?"

"He and his henchman came into the store last week. I stayed in the background. He's an oily one. Didn't actually come out and say he'd do something to the mercantile, but implied it. Made a reference to the barbershop."

"I'm not surprised. It was damaged late last month. Someone broke in and smashed things up. The mirrors, chairs, poked a hole in the water heater tank."

Clay nodded. "I could tell the man was no good as

soon as I saw him. There was another man I saw riding up the street. He had his hat pulled low so I can't give you any more details than that. He's another one I know is up to no good."

Alex leaned forward. "Did he do something suspicious?"

"No, just rode by. I could just tell. It's sort of a talent I have, being able to see if someone has nefarious intent."

"You don't say."

Clay let the topic drop, deciding the marshal might not be ready to hear about his Callings. "I'd like to help you in any way I can to capture these no accounts taking advantage of the townsfolk. I've got some experience in posses and deputy work. The sort where you deputize for a day or so. I'd also be another set of eyes and ears around town."

"So you're not looking for a job."

Clay laughed. "No sir. I've got my hands full with the mercantile, new wife and nine children."

Alex grinned. "I saw a mess of children around you and Mrs. Cutler on Sunday."

Clay grinned back. "Yeah. They are getting along well at the moment. I'm sure there will be some wrangling as time goes on. It comes with the territory."

CHAPTER SIX

"CLAY, WAS THERE ANY CHEWING tobacco in that shipment?" Reuben and Ben heard the question as they set the cans of peaches and cherries on the shelves. Each day they had to do some chores in the mercantile. It peeved them that Opal and Grace didn't have to do them. When the boys had mentioned that to their parents they were met with severe stares, frowns, and the words, "What they have to do is no business of yours. You do as you've been told." They did.

"No, I didn't find any," Clay said, looking over the packing list. "It's not on the list either."

"Well, we only have one more pouch. That'll be gone today, most likely. I'll place another order."

A crash was heard from the apartment, then screams and cries. Ben and Reuben watched as their parents ran past.

"You boys mind the store. We'll be right back," their Pa yelled as he took the stairs two at a time.

Ben and Reuben looked at each other.

"What do you suppose happened?" Ben asked.

"Abe probably fell. It happens a lot."

"That sounded like a pretty bad fall."

Reuben nodded. They continued placing cans on the shelves. A few minutes later their parents came down the stairs and through the store.

"We're taking Abe to Doc and Hattie's. He fell and cut his head open," Mama said, nearly running past them. Pa followed with a screaming Abe in his arms. A towel was held against his head, stained red with blood. "Lock the door and flip the sign to 'Closed.'"

"Ryder and Nate are nailing lath in Fern's room if you need them. Fern and the girls are upstairs," Pa hollered as he ran out the door.

"Okay," Reuben jumped up and followed, doing as he'd been instructed. He looked as they hurried up the street and around the corner. "I hope he's okay," Reuben said, scrunching his eyebrows together.

"Me too," Ben said.

They looked at each other.

"We're almost done with our cans. I think we should figure out some other way we can help. They're going to be gone a while, then worried more about Abe to get much done today." Ben looked around.

"That's a real good idea. We could unpack the shipping crate. That would help," Reuben headed to the back room where their Pa had been working.

Ben followed. "Nah, I think it's too tall for us to reach into."

Reuben eyed the crate. "Yeah, you're right." He picked up the packing list from the floor and looked at it. A smile came over his face as he looked at his new brother. "I have an idea. Come on. Let's get the rest of these cans done while I tell you."

* * *

Millie tried to keep up, but Clay was running faster than she could. She'd told him the doctor's office was across the park so rather than sticking to the street, he cut through. Abe was still crying, his head tucked under Clay's chin.

Clay didn't pause when he reached the office. He glanced back making eye contact with Millie before he wrenched the door open and entered. By the time she got there they were already in an exam room. She didn't wait. She ran right in.

"Looks like you banged yourself up real good there, young man," Dr. Robert Childs was saying as he examined the cut on Abe's scalp. He pushed his glasses up on his nose and looked at Clay. "Can you tell me what happened?"

"Mrs. Cutler and I were downstairs in the mercantile when it happened. We heard a crash, screams, and his cries. We ran upstairs. Abe was on the floor of the kitchen. Fern said he must have climbed up on the counter and fallen. I think his head hit the corner of the table. Abe was lying under it."

"I see. Do you make a habit of leaving a toddler alone?" Censure was evident in the doctor's tone."

"There were several older children up there. He wasn't alone." Clay looked at Millie. She went to stand next to him.

Abe had quit crying and was sucking his thumb. The bleeding seemed to have stopped. He was covered in blood. It made Millie slightly sick to her stomach.

"Well, I'll have to stitch the wound together. It will hurt. I'm sure we'll have to wrap him in a sheet to keep him from struggling." Doc Childs turned, nearly bumping into his wife, Hattie.

Hattie was quite tall for a woman. Not totally accepted in town because she was part Indian. She was an expert in herbals used for healing which also caused some problems with some of the townsfolk. Millie respected Hattie who had helped provide relief from croup for Opal several years ago.

"Hattie, get a sheet while I get what I need to stitch this up." Doc Childs pushed his glasses up again.

Millie picked Abe up, hugging him close. She hated what was going to be done. Last time it was Reuben who needed stitches. His sobs nearly broke her heart. It would be worse with Abe. At least with Reuben she and Sherman had been able to explain why he had to be hurt in order to heal. Abe would never understand.

Hattie brought a large sheet and Millie helped swaddle Abe so only his head was out. Hattie cleaned the wound then smeared a green mush into it. Abe cried and fought the entire time. Millie cried too as she held him against her.

"Can I get a chair for her to sit on? There's no way she'll be able to hold him while Doc puts the stitches in. I'm not sure she'll be able to hold him then." Clay stroked the back of Abe's head. Millie thought his eyes were full of moisture.

Doc nodded as he arranged needles and thread on a cloth covered tray. Clay brought a straight chair from the waiting room.

After shaving around the cut, Doc wiped the green

mush from the cut and cleaned it again. Abe struggled against his mother crying. Tears were streaming down her face. Clay held her shoulders while Doc Childs put seven stitches in the scalp of the small child.

"See, it's real easy." Reuben picked a cigar out of the box and stuck it into the cigar cutter. Thwack, the end fell off into a small bowl. He pushed the cigar in again. Thwack, another chunk fell in the bowl. "We can cut these up and package them. Then there'll be chewing tobacco to sell."

Ben's eyes lit up. "That's a great idea. Let me do the next one." He picked a cigar out of the box while Reuben continued cutting his cigar up. "What are we going to package them in?"

"We can use the bags they put candy in. They're small, just about the same size as the pouches. What do you think?"

"Great idea. How about we write on the bag what's in them? Makes it easy for customers to know what they're getting." Ben stuck his cigar into the cutter. Thwack. Thwack. Thwack.

"I'll get some bags. Shall we write in ink or pencil?" Reuben jumped down from the counter he was sitting on.

"Ink would be better, but I've never written with a pen before." Thwack.

"Me neither, but I think it would look better in ink."

"Yeah." Ben got another cigar from the box. Thwack.

Reuben reached under the counter bringing out a

stack of small brown paper bags. "How many do you suppose we'll need?"

"Depends on how many pieces we put in each one. Get the pouch of chew. We could weigh it and make our bags weigh the same."

"Good idea. That way the price will be the same as the real pouches. We can put that on the bag." Reuben put the bags on the floor, then got a bottle of ink and a fountain pen from beside the cash register. "My turn. You write on the bags."

"Okay." Thwack. Ben put the end of the cigar in the bowl with the other bits. "We need something else to put these in. The bowl's full."

"Just dump them on the floor. We can put them in the bags when we get all done cutting them up." Thwack. Thwack.

Ben dumped the bowl and placed it in its holder on the cigar cutter. "Hey, look at the cigar box. It's got a good picture on it. See, it's a crown. We can draw that too so they know what kind of tobacco it is."

Thwack. "Yeah," Reuben said. Thwack.

Ben lay down on the floor and picked up a pen. "Do you suppose this has ink in it?"

"Try it and see." Thwack.

Pulling a bag toward him, Ben wrote, 'Cheuing Tobbaco.' How's this?" He held up the bag.

"Great, but I think you spelled it wrong."

Ben looked at the pouch of tobacco lying beside him. "Yeah, I did." He frowned and twisted his mouth to the side. "Should I throw it away?"

"Nah. Most of the men who buy that stuff can't read anyway. Now, draw the crown below the writing."

Thwack.

Ben's tongue stuck out of the corner of his mouth as he drew. The crown was lopsided and off-center. He held up the bag for Reuben to see. "How's this?"

"Looks good." Thwack. "Your turn to cut up cigars. I'll write on a bag." Reuben jumped down and Ben climbed up. Thwack.

Half way through writing the pen ran out of ink. "Hey, we need to refill the pen. Do you know how?" Reuben asked.

Ben looked down. "Maybe."

"Same here."

Ben jumped off the counter. "I'll help."

They studied the pen. Reuben twisted the nib, unscrewing it. His fingers turned black. "I've got it open. You put the ink in."

Ben picked up the ink bottle and squeezed the eye-dropper bulb. When he pulled it from the bottle ink dripped onto his trousers. He rubbed the spot with his hand. "Do you suppose it will wash out?" he asked, looking at Reuben.

"Yeah. It's just ink."

"Hold the pen still."

Reuben held the nib in one hand, the base in the other. Ben lined up the eye-dropper over the hole and squeezed. Ink filled the reservoir and overflowed across Reuben's fingers and onto his sock.

"At least the ink is black. Even if it doesn't wash out no one will be able to tell," Ben said. He looked at his dark brown trousers. "Maybe I should paint my trousers black. Do you think Mama would notice?"

"I don't think she'll notice the spot. She'll be too

worried about Abe. Did you see all that blood?"

"Yeah. Do you suppose all his blood will leak out?"

"Nah, I cut my arm last year real bad. See." Reuben pushed his sleeve up showing off his scar. "Papa said I bled like a stuck pig. Doc Henderson had to stitch it up. It hurt like the very devil. Miss Richards put some herb stuff on it before he stitched it. Said it would help with the hurt. If it did I sure couldn't tell."

"Did you cry?"

"Nah. I was tough." Reuben puffed out his chest.

"Really?"

"Well, I may have cried a little."

"I probably would have. A little."

Once the pen was ready, the boys continued cutting up cigars and writing on the bags. When all the cigars were in pieces Reuben brought the small scales to where they were working. They set the pouch of tobacco on one side and a bag on the other. Picking the pieces off the floor, they filled the bag until it balanced, somewhat.

"See, that works real well," Ben said.

"Yeah." Reuben grinned at Ben. "We're a good team. I'm sure Mama and Pa will be real happy. They'll have chewing tobacco to sell."

Ben nodded. "Let's get these bags filled. We can set them on the shelves."

Once the boys were done, they put the pen and ink bottle away, leaving a splotch of black ink on the floor, and with black spotted hands and ink smeared faces, they carefully placed twenty-one bags of cut up cigars on the shelf with one pouch of chewing tobacco.

* * *

Clay carried Abe as he and Millie walked back to the mercantile. Abe was asleep, having cried himself to sleep once the stitches were done and his head wrapped in a bandage. Clay was exhausted and he was sure Millie was too. The stress and worry, as well as all the tears, left him feeling like he'd run ten miles.

They climbed the outside stairs slowly. When Clay stepped into the parlor eight pairs of eyes pinned him.

Opal's eyes filled. Her hands went to her mouth. "Is Abe dead?"

Millie knelt in front of her daughter pulling her into her arms. "No, he's sleeping. He's had a really tough morning."

Opal burst into tears. "I was so afraid he'd die just like Papa did," she sobbed.

Clay laid a hand on Millie's shoulder. "You stay here. I'll put him to bed." She nodded as she comforted Opal. Fern and Reuben cuddled in close to their mother as Clay's children looked on, understanding how they felt.

When Clay returned, the tears were all dry and Fern was telling how she, Opal, and Grace had fixed lunch. They'd boiled eggs, with Ryder carrying the pot of boiling water, and opened cans of pork and beans. Ryder moved that pot, too.

Fern was excited over their accomplishments. "We had those and leftover biscuits and bread and butter. Ida only spilled a little milk but we cleaned it up. We did the dishes. One bowl got broken and a glass, but nobody got cut. There's some eggs left and beans for you but no biscuits because the boys ate them all up." Fern shot a disgusted glance at Ryder and Nate.

Millie hugged all three little homemakers. "Thank you. That was very thoughtful of you."

"Well, the boys were complaining they were hungry. We didn't want to listen to their stomachs growling," Grace said, her hands on her hips. "But they did say thank you, so at least they minded their manners."

Clay bit his lip to keep from laughing. Ida wrapped an arm around his leg. It was her nap time. A nap sounded wonderful to him. Picking her up, he said, "How about I put you to bed?" She nodded and laid her head on his shoulder. As he went down the hall Clay heard Grace and Opal begging not to have to take a nap. He wondered what Millie would do. The girls had been fighting the idea of naps since the wedding. Seems they thought they were too old for them. Maybe they were, but he'd let Millie decide.

When he returned only Millie was in the apartment. She was in the kitchen dishing up the beans. A bowl with several eggs was on the table as well as bread and butter.

"I sent them all to the park. The boys took a baseball and their mitts. The girls took dolls and a quilt to sit on. It gets them out of the house to work off some of their energy and we can take a nap. I'm exhausted." Millie sat down and wiped her hands over her face.

Clay sat and took one of her hands in his. "Me too. I was so scared when I saw all that blood. At least he was crying and not knocked out. I would have been terrified then."

"I know." She looked at him, her eyes reflecting the fear he'd felt. "Clay, I don't know what I would have done if he'd died. I can't lose another one I love.

Sherman's death was so difficult to get through, but I had to go on. The children needed me. The town needed me to be able to supply things they needed to keep going. Everyone went through so much loss. So many people died. So many men just gone all at once.

"We were all just numb, the women who lost husbands and fathers. Suddenly we were all grieving and having to do jobs we knew little or nothing about. I don't know how many times one of the ladies would come in and we'd just start crying when we saw each other. We'd hug and cry.

"It's funny. I felt so alone and yet so very supported by the other ladies. Even ones I didn't know well or have much in common with."

"Grief can bring people together or tear them apart. God's mercy was on Silverpines that he gave you comfort in each other." Clay stroked her cheek.

"I never thought of it that way. As God's mercy during such a tragic time."

"I never did either until Lucy died. Not only did my children and I get closer, but my siblings gathered around and were there for us in so many ways. Sometimes it was just to sit with me, not saying anything. That helped so much. Just knowing they were there and I could cry or stare off into space and they'd be there with me."

"Like Job's friends."

"Yes. I thought of that several times. At least my family didn't go on to tell me it happened because of my sin."

Millie smiled. "That's good." She took a deep breath and straightened her shoulders. "We better get this eaten and take our nap. Abe won't sleep all afternoon. He'll get hungry and wake up."

"And there will be eight more bellies wanting to be filled this evening."

"No, that will be eleven."

Clay chuckled, squeezed her hand and said grace.

CHAPTER SEVEN

RYDER THREW THE BALL TO Reuben who dropped it just like every other time it was thrown to him. Ben wasn't much better. He was getting tired of waiting for them to run and get the ball before they could try to throw it. He knew they were little but this was getting old.

He looked around and saw the girls sitting under the large tree near the corner. Fern and Opal had their dolls. Grace was studying something with her magnifying glass.

Reuben finally threw the ball to Nate who tossed it to Ben who didn't catch it. Ryder sighed. He ran to where Nate was waiting.

"Hey, how about we go fishing? I'm tired of them not catching the ball."

Nate smiled. "Good idea. I suppose we have to take them." He jerked a thumb toward the other boys.

"Yeah, I suppose so. Hey, we can have them dig worms for us." Ryder stuck his arm out and caught the ball Ben threw toward him. He waved them over. "Want to go fishing with us?"

Two faces lit up with delight. "Yeah."

Ryder saw Jackson Hershell wandering aimlessly past the park with his hands in his pockets. He must not have any jobs to do today. Ryder had met the boy soon after they arrived in Silverpines. They were the same age. Jackson was taller than Ryder and stronger. Ryder couldn't decide if he was jealous of that or not. He did like Jackson.

"Hey, Jackson." Ryder waved him over. "You want to go fishing with us?"

"Sure. I've got a pole at home. I'll go get it."

"Great. We'll meet you at the back of the mercantile."

Nate ran over to tell the girls while the others headed for the store. Reuben ran up the outside steps so he could enter and go down the storeroom stairs and open the back door.

"Everything's quiet upstairs," he said as the other boys entered.

They put their ball and mitts on the bottom step then retrieved the fishing poles and creel from behind the staircase. Ryder grabbed the key hanging on a hook beside the door.

"No sense having to go upstairs to come in to put the poles away," Ryder said. Jackson was waiting for them and they headed toward the river.

At the river bank Reuben led them downstream to an inlet lined with trees. The bank dropped off rather than gently sloping to the water.

"Papa and me, we'd come here and fish. He said when Abe got bigger he'd come too." Tears glistened in Reuben's eyes. The other boys nodded but didn't say anything.

A split log was near the river's edge forming two benches. While Ryder and Nate unwound the line and hooks from the bamboo poles, Ben and Reuben got an old serving spoon and tin can out of the creel.

"You guys dig up some worms, will you?" Ryder said.

"Sure." The prospect obviously delighted two eight-year-olds.

It wasn't long before corks floated in the water strung to five poles.

"You suppose we'll catch enough for supper?" Ben asked.

Nate laughed. "That'd take more time than we have unless they are biting well. Besides, do you want to clean all those fish? You know the rule. 'Them what brings them home cleans them.'"

"Yuck," said Reuben. "How about we throw them back instead of taking them home?"

"I hope I catch some. I'll clean them myself and fry them up. Good eating." Jackson rubbed his stomach.

They fell silent waiting for a nibble.

"Well, what have we here?"

The voice had all the boys turning around to see who spoke. Something made Ryder pass his pole to Ben sitting beside him as he stood up.

"We're just fishing," Ryder said.

"You're one of the new kids whose pa married Mrs. Messer, aren't you?" The man was not overly tall, thin with a narrow mustache. His eyes were sunk deep in his head. He ignored Jackson.

Ryder didn't like the man. Something seemed off about him. It wasn't anything he could explain. The man made him uneasy. He nodded.

"Well." The man stretched one side of his mouth into an odd smile. "You boys be careful. You wouldn't want anything to happen to any of you. It'd make your folks real sad if anything harmed you."

Ryder swallowed. "We're being careful, sir. I'll watch out for my brothers."

This time the man nodded.

"I've got a bite," Ben hollered.

Ryder turned his attention from the man to Ben who was pulling up on his pole. He helped Ben land the fish.

"Wow, that's a fine one," Nate said. Reuben agreed.

Once they'd freed the fish from the hook, Ben tossed it back in the water. Ryder turned to look at the man. He was gone. As he helped Ben thread another worm on his hook, Ryder decided to tell his pa about the encounter.

Clay stood looking down at Millie. She was still sleeping. Her face gave evidence of the stress and fear of the events of the morning. They'd only been married about a week. She was still recovering from the pressures she'd been under after the disaster. This would set her back he was sure.

Clay hoped Ida and Abe slept longer. That would give her more rest. He didn't want her to have to cook supper so he planned to send Ryder and Nate to the cafe to purchase their meal.

Checking on Abe, Clay found him sound asleep sucking on his thumb. Not wanting to wake him he refrained from stroking the soft cheek. Abe was such a sweet, easy baby. Not at all like any of his boys. They'd all been active, demanding, fussbudgets. He smiled at the memories.

He peeked in on Ida. She was sleeping too. Checking his pocket watch, he figured she might sleep another hour. He'd be sure to come back up in plenty of time so she wouldn't wake Millie if she were still asleep.

Clay went down into the mercantile. The canned goods Ben and Reuben were shelving when Abe fell were all neatly placed with their labels facing forward. Well done. He'd have to remember to compliment them.

Moving behind the counter Clay noticed a black splotch on the floorboard that hadn't been there before. Smaller spots were scattered around it. What had happened here? He looked around. Everything seemed to be in order. What was that?

On the shelf where tobacco products were held sat one pouch of chewing tobacco and three neat rows of small brown paper bags closed with Hotchkiss staples. The bags were spotted with ink, crooked letters, and an uneven crown.

Glancing around, Clay saw a box next to the cigar cutter. He picked it up. The weight told him it was empty.

Clay didn't know whether to laugh or be angry. Seems a couple of boys tried to help with the lack of chew available for sale. Too bad they chose to cut up the most expensive cigars in the store.

His mouth stretched into a huge grin. He set the box down and picked up one of the bags. A chuckle burst forth. The ingenuity Ben and Reuben showed made Clay wonder what their teenage years would be like. He hoped Millie saw it in the same light as he did.

She was certainly a beautiful woman. He loved when she brushed out her hair. It was the color of fine dark mahogany wood and flowed in waves down her back. He longed to run his hands through it to see if it was as soft as it looked.

Clay knew it was too soon. Her husband had only been gone two months. Plus she was still worn out from those two months. Lucy had been gone six months now and all he'd done was move his family from Colorado to Oregon. Clay was going to have to wait to reveal his attraction to her.

Forcing those thoughts from his mind, Clay pulled the ledgers out and placed them on the counter. He hadn't had time to look at them yet. He and Millie had gone to the bank opening a new account with both their names. They were changing the name of the store to Silverpines Mercantile. Both wanted to provide for their children. With the money he brought from his sale of his portion of Cutler General Store they would be able to expand when Ryder was ready and then Nate. If things worked well there should be opportunities for all the children.

Opening the ledger marked Credit Accounts he found what Millie had told him. The entries on each page before the earthquakes were itemized with totals for each date and payments listed in a neat hand. After they continued for several entries neat but in a different handwriting, Millie's. Then the writing became sloppy. Finally only the date and total purchase was listed.

There were pages that had no entries after the middle of April. Clay realized these families either died or had left Silverpines. Only a few showed that there had been a payment made on the account. As sympathetic as he was to the people who had suffered so drastically, Clay knew he would have to begin asking for payments on the accounts. He'd speak to Millie about who could pay the complete amount and those who would be helped by partial payments on their account.

Next he looked in the Orders ledger. Again, order entries went from itemized neatly and totaled to sloppy with just a total. Stuffed in the book were packing slips and order invoices. Some were cross-checked. Others just put together.

Clay realized more fully what Millie had been going through having to run the store as well as tend her children. The entries in the Credit Accounts showed how busy the store had been in the days following the disaster.

So many household items were being replaced. Millie had ordered dishes, glasses, many items that would have been damaged or broken during the earthquakes. Few had arrived before June when the railroad began running again. There were empty crates still in the back room when he arrived. Clay, Ryder, and Nate broke them down the first few days.

Hearing footsteps coming down the stairs, Clay looked up seeing Millie carrying Abe with Ida next to her coming from the back room. Ida ran to him with a smile. She reached up so he gathered her into his arms.

"Did you have a good nap, missy?"

"And snack. We had applesauce and toast."

"Sounds good." Clay looked at Millie and Abe. He had his head on her shoulder. "Hi, buddy. How are you feeling?"

Abe pointed to his head. "Owie."

"I'll bet." He looked at Millie then at the jar with lollipops. She nodded with a smile. He pulled two from the jar. "Here." He gave one to each child, even getting a smile from Abe.

"Tank you," Ida said around the candy in her mouth.

Millie set Abe on his feet. He and Ida went to the low windows on the front of the store and looked at the passing traffic.

"Come look at this. We have a couple of precocious eight-year-olds." Clay moved and pointed at the floor. Millie came around the counter.

"What?"

"Seems they wanted to help by supplying us with chewing tobacco to sell." Clay picked up the empty cigar box then pointed to the shelf of brown bags.

Millie looked from the floor to the box and the shelf. Her lips twitched. Then she began laughing. Clay realized it was the first time he'd ever heard her laugh. The beautiful sound flipped his heart over. He vowed it wouldn't be the last.

The next morning Clay was mixing plaster while Nate and Ryder nailed lath to the studs in the room that would be Fern's. He sent Nate for another bucket of water as he stirred the stiff mixture.

"Pa," Ryder said as he came to stand next to him.

Clay looked up and raised an eyebrow.

"Yesterday when we were fishing that man who spoke to you when we were eating after you married Mama came up. He— well, I just had a funny feeling about him."

"What kind of feeling?"

"That I didn't like him. That what he said wasn't what he thought."

"What did he say?"

"He told us to be careful. That you wouldn't want anything to happen to us. That you'd be real sad if anything happened."

"All that's true."

"I know, but I don't think that's what he meant. I think he wants something to happen. That he'd like something to happen." Ryder paused. "I think he might even want to hurt one or more of us."

Clay stopped stirring. "I think you're right. That's Mr. Terhall. He's not a good man. He's asking people to pay him so nothing bad happens. If they don't he's likely to damage their homes or businesses."

"Did he do that to Mama?"

"Yes."

"Did she pay?"

"No."

"Will something bad happen to us?"

"Not if I can help it. I had the same feeling about the man as you had when I first saw him. It was the feeling of a Calling. I think you just had your first Calling."

Ryder's eyes lit up. "You think so?"

"Yes, I do. It's not something you need to do anything about. It was just a feeling of distrust, am I right?" Clay watched his son carefully.

"Yes, just a feeling."

"You remember that feeling. It'll come when God

wants to warn you about someone. Usually it's not a good person. If He wants you to act you'll know. It'll draw you and you'll know where to go and maybe what's going to happen. I can't really explain it better than that. You'll just know God wants you to act on it. If you doubt it then do nothing. Consider it a warning."

Ryder nodded.

"Have you told anyone else about your feeling?"

"No. I wanted to talk with you first. You told us, Nate, Ben, and me, not to talk about the Callings and if we ever felt one to talk to you."

"Good. You did right. Don't tell Nate. Don't tell any of the others. I'll tell your mama when the time is right. She'll need to know eventually, but until I get the Call from God to tell her I won't. She's got enough to handle right now without that."

"Okay."

"I'm proud of you, son. Know one thing. No matter how you feel about a Calling, it's a blessing from God and to be taken seriously. At times you won't think it's a blessing but it is. It enables us to help others, keeping evil people from their deeds, and good people from harm."

CHAPTER EIGHT

IDA HELD THE RAIL AS she followed Opal, Fern, and Grace down the stairs. She thought about Opal's birthday that was in a few days. She didn't know how but Ida wanted to give her something.

Opal was a good new sister. She didn't mind playing with Ida. Not like Grace who always wanted to look at things with her magnifying glass. Especially bugs. Yuck. Grace turned them over with her finger and watched their legs wobble. Ida didn't like bugs. And Grace didn't let her look through the glass.

Maybe she could take a lollipop out of the jar and give it to Opal. No, the jar was too high for her to reach. They sure were good though and she knew Opal really liked candy. She got in trouble a lot for taking a lemon drop. At least when she wasn't caught she'd give one to Ida too. And Grace, but she didn't count.

"Take my hand, Ida," Fern said as they stepped into the street. They were headed to the park. Ida was glad today was sunny. It had rained for several days and they'd had to stay in the apartment. Fern got crabby when that happened. She was okay as a sister but not as good as Opal.

Mama was good too but she was busy a lot. She went down to the store most mornings and didn't come up until it was time to fix lunch. Then she put Ida and Abe to bed for their naps. That's when Pa went to the store. In the mornings he was upstairs but banged in the new rooms they were building for Fern and the older boys.

Ida missed her ma. She had always had time to read to Ida and Grace. She sewed them dresses that were alike and made ones for their dolls too. Pa had brought Ma's sewing machine when they moved but Mama didn't sew. At least Ida didn't think she did. Mama worked in the store, the kitchen, and washed clothes. Ida wished Mama had time to just hold her. She held Abe more but he was still a baby really. And he had cut his head open. He still had a bandage wrapped around his head.

"There's my friend Betty. You all go play under the tree. I'm going to play with Betty over there." Fern pointed across the park.

Ida watched her go. She didn't want to play dolls. She wanted to run. She ran to the tree and seated her doll against the trunk. Opal and Grace sat down and began to play. Ida ran to the bushes and back. Then she ran all the way across to where Fern was and back.

"It was really nice of Reuben to try to get me a kitty but it was bad at the same time. Reuben almost died. I want a kitty but not so anybody would die. He was real upset about it." Ida listened to Opal. She could tell Opal wanted a kitty really badly.

Ida turned and ran across the park again. The sun was warm and white flowers were blooming on the bushes.

She ran to them wanting to smell their sweet scent.

"Mew, mew, mew."

Ida bent down to see under the branches.

"Mew, mew, mew."

She got down on her knees. A kitten came forward on wobbly legs. It was grey and black striped with white chest and legs. It rubbed against Ida, purring loudly. She looked at Opal and Grace. They were playing with their dolls. Grace took her magnifying glass from her pocket and looked at something in the grass. She had Opal look too.

Ida petted the kitten. She smiled. She had the perfect thing for Opal for her birthday. Picking up the kitten, Ida crossed the street and slowly climbed the stairs. It was hard since she couldn't hold the railing. When she opened the door the kitten nearly escaped from her arms, but Ida managed to get it into the apartment.

The door to the storeroom where Pa, Ryder, and Nate were working on the new bedrooms was closed. Mama didn't want the plaster dust making a mess in the apartment. She knew Ben and Reuben were doing chores in the store and Mama was keeping Abe close while he still had his head wrapped up. Ida was alone. She could put the kitty under her bed and keep it there until Opal's birthday.

In the bedroom, she put the kitty down. It began looking around, then ran under Opal's bed. Ida thought that was okay since no one could see it. Now she needed to find some food. She closed the door and went to the kitchen.

Mama had cooked chicken yesterday to make some kind of casserole today. It was all in small pieces since

Mama had picked it already. Ida didn't know how picking out a chicken to cook would make it into small bits, but it would make it easy to get some for the kitty.

First she had to open the icebox. The handle was hard for her to lift but she pulled hard and it opened. The bowl with the chicken was on the bottom shelf covered with a plate. Ida was careful not to drop the plate when she took several bits of meat from the bowl. With the plate back on top, she closed the icebox, dropping the chicken as she pushed.

When she got back to the bedroom, the kitty was at the door crying. It began purring when Ida entered. She put the chicken under her bed. The kitten ran over and started eating. Ida smiled. She had the perfect thing to give Opal for her birthday.

Millie looked up when she heard footsteps clattering down the stairs. Clay was followed by Ryder and Nate. She grinned. The boys looked haggard.

"I don't ever want to plaster a ceiling again. My arms are nearly dead," Nate complained.

"Mine too." Ryder plopped down on the chair sitting next to a barrel with a checkerboard on it.

"One more to do, my boys. The one for your room unless you just want rafters above you." Clay ruffled Ryder's head. Nate ducked the hand that went for his head and flopped to the floor.

"So Fern's room is done, at least the plastering?" Millie asked.

Clay came around the counter and placed his hand on

her back. Warmth spread through her even though several layers including her corset separated his skin from hers. Millie didn't want to admit it to herself but she was becoming attracted to her husband. She still wasn't ready to move their relationship into a more physical range. She mourned Sherman and was just too tired at night. All she wanted was to crawl into bed and sleep.

She had to admit that having a man sleeping next to her felt good. More than good. Being able to reach out in the night and touch him brought comfort and security.

"Yes. We'll start plastering the boys' room tomorrow. Doing that will give Fern's time to dry before we paint it. It should be done and ready early next week if the weather holds. If it gets rainy or damp it will take longer."

"Rain or damp in western Oregon? Does it ever do that?" Millie chuckled. The boys joined her.

"Why don't you go see if the girls want to come home? You could use some sun and air yourself." Clay touched her cheek, letting his finger slide down her skin. Millie only just stopped the shiver threatening to run through her. She stepped away and looked at Clay. The twinkle in his eyes told her she hadn't kept her reaction to herself.

"I'll do that. Then I'll finish fixing lunch." She stepped away and picked up the hat she kept behind the counter. Millie looked at the boys around the checkerboard. There were four now all looking at her with wide eyes. Heat flamed her cheeks and she hurried out the door.

Scanning the park, Millie counted the girls. There were four but one wasn't hers. It was Betty, Fern's best friend. Where was Ida? Her heart began to race. Where was Ida? Millie hurried across the street and ran to where Fern and Betty were playing.

"Where's Ida?" she yelled.

Fern and Betty looked up at her wide-eyed. "She's playing with Opal and Grace," Fern said.

"No, she's not. She's not in the park. How could you be so careless? She's not yet three. She has to be watched. I trusted you to do that." Millie's voice was tight with anger. She stomped across to Opal and Grace. The beating of her heart loud in her head.

This was awful. To have one of her children missing terrified her. She'd gone through it with Reuben a few weeks after the earthquake. He'd nearly drowned trying to rescue a kitten he wanted to give Opal. Reverend Bates had died saving her son. Reuben had nightmares afterward and was riddled with guilt over the pastor's death.

Her stomach was in knots when she neared the girls. Why would such a thing happen to one of Clay's children? How could she tell him his youngest daughter was missing?

"Where's Ida?" Millie fell to her knees searching Opal's and Grace's faces desperately hoping they had an answer for her.

"I don't know, Mama. She was running back and forth between us and Fern." Opal's eyes were wide with fear. Grace had tears running down her face.

"Grace, run and get your pa. I'm going to keep looking." As the girl jumped up and ran off Millie stood and began searching the bushes calling for Ida. Maybe she'd gotten tired and fallen asleep.

Millie was sobbing Ida's name when a little voice said, "I'm right here, Mama."

Jerking around, Millie saw the strawberry locks on the bottom step of the stairs leading to the apartment. She ran across the street and grabbed Ida into a big hug. She kissed the small head over and over.

Arms came around them both. "What happened?" Clay asked. "Grace came in crying that Ida was lost."

"I— I came over to get the girls but Ida wasn't in the park. Fern hadn't been watching her. Opal and Grace didn't know where she was. I called and called. Just now she answered from here on the steps."

Clay took Ida's chin in his hand. "Where did you go? Why didn't you tell Fern or Grace where you were going?"

"I couldn't. I had to take Opal's birthday present up to my room to hide it. I didn't want to spoil the surprise."

"Her birthday present?" Clay asked.

"Yeah. I found it in the park. I can't tell 'cause it's a secret."

By now Grace and Opal were next to them.

Clay took Ida from Millie, kissed her and set her down. "You three go up to the apartment. We'll be up in a few minutes to get lunch ready."

Millie looked around for Fern. She was nowhere in sight. "Oh, Clay. I yelled so at Fern. I called her irresponsible. I'm sure I hurt her feelings. She's not irresponsible. Not at all. I was just so scared for Ida. After the earthquakes, losing Sherman, and almost losing Reuben, I knew I wouldn't be able to stand losing another one I love." She was weeping from the fear and now from her unfair anger at Fern. "She's been so wonderful to take on the girls and Abe so much for me. I know she needs more time to play and just be a little girl. I was so unfair to her."

Clay gathered her against him. He kissed her forehead. "It's okay. She'll spend some time alone and then come home. You can apologize to her then. She'll forgive you. As soon as the rooms are done I'll have more time in the store. So will Ryder and Nate. That will ease your schedule. Then Fern can go play on her own."

"I hope she'll forgive me. I was just so scared I'd lose your daughter." She laid her head against his shoulder. He felt so strong and steady with his arms around her. He gave her hope she hadn't destroyed Fern with her hastily thrown words.

"Let's close the store until after lunch. Or better yet, let the boys handle it. We'll be upstairs if they need us. I'll help you fix lunch." He kissed her forehead again then guided her up the stairs.

Fern ran past the church and into the cemetery. Throwing herself onto her father's grave she wept, sobbing her heart out.

"I didn't mean to lose Ida. I just wanted to play with Betty. I haven't been able to since you died, Papa. All I do is watch the girls and Abe. Mama's been so mean to me. I can't ever do what I want anymore. I can't ever just be alone. Always Opal or Grace or Ida or Abe or even one of the boys is always there. There's just too many of them. Mama never reads to us or plays or takes us to the river anymore. All she does is work and tell me I have to take care of the little ones." She stopped when a gentle hand was laid on her shoulder. Looking up, Fern saw Mrs. Edmondson kneeling beside her.

"You having a bad day?"

"It's been bad ever since Papa died."

"It's been that way for many here in Silverpines." Mrs. Edmondson stood. "Come, let's sit on the bench under the tree over here."

Fern followed her and sat beside the late pastor's wife. They sat in silence for a while. Fern peeked up at Mrs. Edmondson.

"Lovely day today. Warm and sunny. We need to thank the Lord for days like today." Mrs. Edmondson was looking at the puffy clouds lazily passing by in the sky.

Fern just sat in silence.

"We've not had many lovely days since the earthquake even when the weather is good. Silverpines isn't what it used to be. Everyone has so much sorrow and grief to get through. So much work to do to rebuild the town and their lives. So much work."

Fern looked up at her. "Mama works all the time. I thought when she married Pa she'd have time for us again. That I wouldn't have to watch Opal and Abe anymore. But now I have to watch them and Grace and Ida. It's not fair."

"Who told you life was fair?"

Fern pulled her eyebrows together. "Isn't it supposed to be?"

"Was it fair for the mine to collapse and the mudslide that killed so many? Was it fair that your Pa's first wife died of pneumonia? Was it fair that Jesus died on the cross to take our sins away?"

Fern shook her head. "No."

"Is it fair that your mama has so much work to do that she can't take time to play with you or mind her own children and those of her new husband?"

"No."

"Is it fair that you have been asked to help your mama so she can get her work done?"

Fern looked up, wondering how she was supposed to answer that question.

"No," said Mrs. Edmondson. "But that's life. We have to do things we don't want to do. Have to accept that things aren't fair. We also can know that the Holy Spirit is there for us for our comfort. To take our tears and put them in bottles because they are precious to God."

Fern nodded. Pastor James had spoken about that in church a while back. "Mama was really scared about Ida being gone."

"I'm sure she was."

"She's never yelled at me like that before, not even when I spilled milk all over Abe when I tripped over him when he crawled in front of me. It was a big glass too. It broke into a million pieces."

Mrs. Edmondson grinned. "She's a good mama and now she has nine children to take care of instead of four. And she has to work in the store, too."

"Pa says it won't be much longer until the bedrooms are done and he can work in the store more."

"Bedrooms?"

"Yeah, he's building two rooms. One for the boys and one for me so I don't have to sleep in with the little girls."

"That's real thoughtful of him."

"Mama wanted me to have the room. I think it was her idea."

"Real nice of your mama."

"Yes." Fern was silent for a moment. "I might miss the little girls some."

"You might for a while, but I figure you'll like it pretty well most of the time."

"Do you suppose they found Ida?"

"I imagine she didn't go very far."

"I think I'll go home and find out. If they haven't, I want to go help look for her."

"That's a good idea."

Fern jumped off the bench and took two steps. She turned around and gave Mrs. Edmondson a hug. "Thank you."

Mrs. Edmondson hugged her back, then smiled as Fern ran toward home.

Hearing someone running up the stairs, Millie looked out the window that overlooked them. The top of Fern's dark blonde head passed by. She was the only one of their children with Sherman's coloring. Her eyes were the same deep blue of an autumn sky.

Millie exited the kitchen just as Fern burst into the parlor.

"Did you find Ida?"

"Yes, sweetie, we did." Millie came and wrapped her arms around Fern. "She had come up to the apartment to hide the gift for Opal's birthday she found in the park.

"I'm so sorry I yelled at you like I did. I didn't mean

anything I said. I was so scared and I took it out on you. You've been such a wonderful help to me. You've been so responsible in taking care of the little ones since…" She stopped. No sense explaining that. Fern knew. "It won't be long before you won't have to do it anymore."

"I know, Mama. I'm sorry I didn't watch Ida better. I just got to playing with Betty and I forgot."

Millie stroked her hair. "I know. But you know what? By this time next week the rooms will be done and Pa can work the store more. So will Ryder and Nate. You'll not have to mind the little ones."

Fern smiled. "That'll be good. They get real tiring to be around so much. Ida always wants to look in Grace's magnifying glass and she won't let her. Then Ida gets mad or cries."

"I promise you won't have to watch them."

"I will sometimes. They can be fun. Just not all the time."

Millie kissed Fern's head. "No, not all the time."

A scream, then another came down the hall from the girls' room. One was Opal's. The other was from Grace. Millie and Fern looked at each other and ran down the hall. Clay came out of Abe's room carrying him after changing his diaper.

Millie opened the door, running into the bedroom. "What's happened?"

Opal and Grace stood on the bed, eyes wide with fear. Ida was looking under the bed. She turned and Millie saw big tears rolling down her face.

"It was supposed to be a surprise for her birthday. Now it's not a surprise."

Millie sat on the floor and gathered Ida into her lap.

"What's not a surprise?"

"The kitty."

Millie looked up at Clay. He shrugged.

"What kitty?"

"The one I found in the park and brought home for Opal. He came out from under the bed. They screamed and scared him. He's in the corner all shivering." Ida buried her face in Millie's bosom and sobbed.

Clay put Abe down and rounded the bed. Peeking under he found the kitten beside the headboard. He grabbed it and brought it to his chest. "This is the reason for all the screams and tears?"

"Oooo." Grace brought out her magnifying glass, looking at the furry animal in Clay's arms.

"A kitty." Opal clapped. "For me?"

"I found it in the bushes. It was for your birthday. But it's ruined now." Ida sobbed.

Millie looked at Clay. *Just what we need. A kitten,* she thought.

"What are you going to name it?" Fern asked. "Ida, that's a real good present. Opal has wanted a kitten for a long time."

Millie was thankful Fern didn't mention the one Reuben had tried to get for his sister.

Clay put the cat on the bed after Fern and Ida clambered onto it. The four girls were delighted with the gray and white puffball. Abe stood looking at it, as confusion filled his face. Clay helped Millie to her feet and drew her out into the hall.

"It looks like we now have a kitten as well as nine children," she said. "There's no way to take it away from them. We'd have more tears and I don't think I can handle that today."

Clay pulled her into their bedroom and closed the door. "No, not a good idea at all." He wrapped his arms around her.

Millie sighed and leaned against him. She was so glad he'd answered her advertisement. He was the strength she needed. Tipping her head back, she looked into his eyes. "I'm glad it was you who wrote such wonderful letters. You've become my strength, my helpmate." She touched his cheek.

Clay searched her eyes. Then lowered his head, pressing his lips against hers. Desire shot through Millie. It was so strong it startled her. She drew back. Seeing the question in his eyes she knew everything was up to her. He would never pressure her into more than she could give. The question was, was she ready to become his wife in fact as well as name? Millie wasn't sure of the answer.

Pounding sounded on the door. Clay stepped back and opened it. Opal stood there holding the kitten with her brother and sisters behind her.

"I decided on a name for the kitty. It's Kitty 'cause it's a kitty."

Clay lay in bed looking up at the ceiling. Moonlight streamed through the lace curtains at the windows of their bedroom. Something needed to change. Millie was still overworked, stressed, and overwhelmed. He'd thought the rooms would be done by now. Working with two untrained boys slowed down the progress.

He'd known adding five children to Millie's family would up the workload, but he hadn't realized the total of what she'd been dealing with after the earthquakes. Guilt rode hard on him.

The bed started shaking slightly. Clay looked over at Millie. She lay on her side facing away from him. The movement of her shoulders was evidence of her crying. It broke his heart. She never complained. She simply kept going.

Rolling over he pressed against her back, wrapping his arm around her. "Shhh. It's going to be okay."

"I know. In my weakness, He is strong." Millie took a shuddery breath.

"Millie, I'm sorry. I've not eased your burden at all. All I've done is add my children onto your shoulders."

She rolled so she faced him within his arms. "No, I love your children. They are a wonderful addition to mine. You and Lucy did a marvelous job raising them. I'm delighted that they all get along so well."

Clay smiled. "A few minor squabbles aside, they have been very good together. Thank the Lord for that. We certainly don't need bickering on top of everything else." He placed a hand on the back of her head and tucked it under his chin. "Things are going to change. We need less going on."

"Why?"

Clay was pleased when Millie relaxed against him. He hugged her more tightly to him. "I need to be in the store more to get to know it and go over the ledgers and orders so I know them better. We need to figure out what needs to be ordered so we'll have the supplies people need to rebuild, restock, and get their lives back.

"As a family we need some time to relax together. You and your children have gone through a major upheaval. So have mine. Ever since we arrived you and I have been so busy we've not had time to interact with our own children let alone get to know the others well. We need to. It's summer. Now's the time we should be doing some recreational things as a family."

"But how can we do that? The rooms…" Clay stopped her words with fingers on her lips.

"As soon as Fern's room is done the rest will just have to wait. The boys don't care that they are in the storeroom. We're getting along without the bathing room. It can wait. We, as a family, can't.

"We're also going to set regular hours for the store so people know when we'll be open. For the rest of the summer, we'll be closed on Wednesdays. That will give us a chance to have some outings as a family. We need that. You need that."

Millie slipped her arm around his waist. "That sounds wonderful."

"I think we need to make a play area in the back room so the children can be downstairs if we both need to be in the store or one of us has to go somewhere. The piles in there are all gone now so there is room. That will free Fern from having to tend them all the time."

"She'll appreciate that." Millie yawned. "I think all your ideas are just what we need."

Clay tipped her chin up and placed a gentle kiss on her lips. "It's all going to work out well. You'll see. Sleep now."

"I think you're right."

When Millie snuggled to his chest, Clay smiled in the

darkness and closed his eyes.

CHAPTER NINE

A PARTY WAS HELD FOR Opal's birthday with Kitty wearing a red bow that was normally used on the tree at Christmas. Fern and Millie made a chocolate cake that was gone quickly though evidence of it was on several young faces.

Fern's bedroom was painted pink as were four boys who decided flinging paint from brushes at each other was great fun. Fortunately it was done in the storeroom where little damage occurred. Their blankets would forever be spotted pink. The boys spent the next few days scrubbing the walls, floor, and crates of the storeroom. Though the paint didn't wash away, years of grime did. Their next job was washing the back room so a play area could be created.

The choice of fabric for Fern's curtains was difficult. She waffled between blue flowers on pink, and pink and yellow flowers on green. Grace and Opal voiced their opinions which were opposed and resulted in a quarrel. Fern finally chose yellow stripes with pink flowers. Millie opened the sewing machine Clay brought from Stones Creek and soon the window was decorated and two pillow cases made to match.

In the midst of all the cleaning and sewing the family's first Wednesday outing was held. Millie packed a picnic lunch and everyone carried something to the river. Just downriver from town the river split around an island. There was a sand beach along the river's edge where swimming was enjoyed by many of the townsfolk. Today, the Cutlers had the area to themselves, allowing them to spread out so those who wanted to dig holes in the sand could and those whose choice was to build sand castles weren't bothered. Between the groups Millie and Clay spread out blankets and watched the children frolic in the water.

"Ida told me she wanted pie for her birthday," Millie said as she settled on the blanket.

"It's hard for me to realize she'll be three come Friday." Clay dusted some sand off his pant leg then lay back on his elbows. "It seems like only yesterday Lucy told me she was expecting."

"Same with Abe. His birthday is in December. The rest of mine have already happened this year." Millie watched Reuben and Ben splash water on Nate who gave chase, splashing after them and laughing.

"Nate will be twelve in August." They continued discussing and learning the birthdays of all the children. "When is your birthday?" Clay asked.

"September ninth. I'll be thirty." Millie refrained from saying she had never thought she'd be a widow before she attained that age.

"We're hungry." Opal fell on the blanket next to Millie. Grace held Abe by the hand. Ida jumped up to them spraying sand on Clay.

That effectively ended their quiet conversation as the rest of the children gathered around for food.

Clay looked back toward town. Something was going to happen. He didn't know what or when, but his Callings were never wrong. He prayed it wasn't another earthquake. Silverpines was slowly recovering. They didn't need more damage or the reminder of what they'd lost.

Abe climbed onto Clay's lap. He looked funny with part of his head shaved. The stitches were out and the cut healing. Maybe he'd take the boy to the barber and have the rest of the hair shaved off.

The tingle of the Calling faded so Clay put it aside. He'd know when and what in God's timing. It wasn't something he could force.

As Millie rolled out the dough for Ida's birthday pies she thought about how caring Clay was. He'd embraced her children just as she had his. His work to build the needed bedrooms impressed her. She hadn't known he was a carpenter as well as a shopkeeper.

Fern was happy with her new room. Clay had been right that the boys didn't care that their room wasn't going to be finished yet. The pink paint spots didn't please Millie but now the storeroom and the back room were clean, and the play area set up and being used. It freed Fern from child care duty and also gave Millie the opportunity to work either upstairs or in the mercantile.

After they all finished swimming and eating, the family had gone to several houses where no one lived anymore and picked cherries off the trees and blueberries from bushes. Millie didn't see any reason for them to go to waste.

Yesterday she'd tried to get the boys to help pit the cherries. They lasted for about a cup each then thought of chores they needed to do down in the store. Abe wasn't any help but he kept her company as did Kitty who played with a ball of paper under the table.

It seemed to Millie that Clay was touching her in more ways and more often. At first he'd just place his hand on her back as they walked somewhere together. Next he'd place an arm across the back of the settee in the evenings as they sat in the parlor. Now he held her hand at times or touched her shoulder. That night after not knowing where Ida was he'd held her in his arms while she cried. She'd wrapped her arm around him. And he'd kissed her.

Millie thought she could still taste his lips when she licked hers. It was silly of course. It was almost two weeks ago.

The budding desire she felt for him was both welcome and distressing. She knew Sherman was gone and he would want her to be a complete wife to Clay, but she missed him terribly. She was sure Clay missed Lucy. How could he not? They'd loved each other just as she and Sherman had.

Millie smiled to herself. She had wonderful memories. She could share them with her children. Clay would do the same. They would create new memories as the time progressed. She realized she was looking forward to building memories with Clay and his children. She also realized she was looking forward to building memories of just the two of them. But she'd let Clay take the lead on that.

As she was spooning pie filling into the crust Nate came running in. "Mama, Pa needs you to come tend the store. He's gotta go somewhere."

"Where?" Millie washed her hands and picked up Abe.

"He didn't say. Just strapped on his gun belt and ran out the door."

Clay closed the cash drawer and said goodbye to Miss Edie and Miss Ethel Howard. They ran a girls' orphanage and school in town. Sweet spinsters who lived in a large house on the edge of town.

Ryder and Nate were moving stock from one side of the store to another. He and Millie had decided to do some rearranging, looking to add more variety to the store. New products were coming available all the time and they wanted to be able to stock them. Ben and Reuben were putting canned goods on the shelves. That was a good job for two precocious boys. Once they were done he'd release them all to go play outdoors.

Clay was jotting down something needing ordering when the Calling struck him hard and strong. "Nate, run upstairs and get your Mama. I need to head out for a bit." Clay grabbed the gun belt he kept in a box on a high shelf behind the counter. Nate ran to do as he was told while Clay looked at Ryder. "It's a Calling. Strong and urgent. Don't say anything to anyone. Nate will figure it out but tell him to keep quiet about it. I'll be back as soon as I can."

Clay ran out the door as a wide-eyed Ryder nodded.

Running up Main Street, Clay glanced around. He was headed to the jail to talk with Marshal Sewell. There was a slight glow around the bank. He knew no one else could see it and it wouldn't be there later. It was the Calling. Something was going to happen at the bank. Most likely a robbery.

Miss Tilde Lasek was running the bank now since the death of her father and brother in the earthquake. She was young and struggling to understand the intricacies of banking. Clay's Calling showed she would be harmed or worse when outlaws came to do their evil.

Pulling the door to the jail open, Clay rushed in. "There's going to be a bank robbery. Soon."

Marshal Alex Sewell and Deputy Gene Autry jumped up from their seats behind their desks.

"What? How do you know?" Marshal Sewell asked.

"It'll take a little bit of explaining. You know of Nugget Nate Ryder and The Preacher?"

"Everybody does," said Autry.

"Nate was my great-uncle and Nathan is my second cousin. Callings run in my family. My Grandma Aggie had them for girls in need. Mine are not as strong as Nugget Nate's or The Preacher's, but when I get them I know, and right now I know some outlaws are getting ready to rob the bank and harm Miss Lasek."

"Gene, run, get Mason Dekum at the gun shop. He'll help." As the deputy left Alex continued. "My other deputies are out at Bennett's ranch. They were needing some help with some colts and the deputies used to work there."

Clay nodded.

"So, you're a relative of the Ryders of Kentucky. I lived on Ryder Mountain until I was sixteen. I know all the stories. They're told and retold at just about every gathering. I understand all about the Callings. Some of the Ryders on the mountain still have them."

"Yes, Nugget Nate and Aunt Penny came to Stones Creek several times while I was growing up. I have the very knife Jim Bowie used." Clay chuckled. "So do each of my brothers and any other boy Nate gave one to over the years. Nathan came some too when he was with Uncle Nate in the summers."

Alex laughed. "Nathan told me a number of stories about his grandfather. Kept me laughing until my sides ached."

"You should have heard them from the man himself. One thing I'll say is that his versions of the tales of his and my grandmother's growing up years differ tremendously. Especially the tale about the skunk."

Deputy Autry and Mason Dekum came in then. Marshal Sewell deputized Clay and Mason and they made plans to stake out the bank. It wasn't long before three men on horses stopped at the bank.

"Those men were part of Little's gang," Gene said. "They tried to take over the town before Marshal got here. Pretty much succeeded too."

"I thought they died in the mudslide," Sewell said. "Must not have been at the camp when it happened. Never thought they'd come back to town. Gene, you head around back to keep them from escaping that way. We'll enter and stop them."

They gave the deputy time to get in place then ran across the street and into the bank.

One outlaw had Tilde Lasek in his arms trying to kiss her while the other two were putting money into a canvas sack.

"Stop, you're under arrest. Let go of Miss Lasek," Marshal Sewell yelled.

Clay and Mason fanned out to cover each outlaw with their guns. Caught red-handed the thieves gave up without shots being fired. It wasn't long and they were in jail and Miss Lasek was escorted home. Too nervous to keep it open, she closed the bank for the day.

Clay walked back to the mercantile pleased with how everything went down. He thanked God that no shots were fired and no one was hurt. He doubted many townsfolk even knew there had been an attempted robbery at the bank.

Millie rushed to him as he entered the store. "What happened? Where have you been? Nate said you took your guns and just ran out."

He glanced around. No customers were there and no children either. "There were three men trying to rob the bank. I helped the marshal stop it. They are in jail and Miss Lasek is at home, scared but safe."

"What?" Millie shrieked. "Why would you be involved in something like that? Something so dangerous."

"I was needed to help stop the evil those men wanted to do. Miss Lasek was already being accosted when we went in. She could have been hurt or worse, taken by those men." Clay pulled her into his arms, hugging her to him. She relaxed some.

"Poor Tilde. She's had such a difficult time since the earthquake. Her mother doesn't know anything about the bank and refuses to learn. Tilde was a teller before but now has all the responsibility for the bank."

"Has she advertised for a husband?" Clay asked.

"She didn't when the rest of us did. I don't know if she has since then. If she hasn't this might make her think about it more seriously." Millie pulled back and looked at Clay. "That doesn't tell me how you got involved in it."

Clay wasn't comfortable telling her about the Callings. They weren't close enough for him to be sure she would take him seriously when he explained about them. He didn't want to lie to her though. "I just had an inkling something was going to happen. I went to the Marshal's office and helped them capture the outlaws."

"But how did you know?" Millie pressed.

"God just laid it on my heart and I had to obey right then."

Millie just looked at him. Her eyes spoke questions he didn't want to answer. Then they darkened with worry.

"What if something had happened to you? What if you were hurt badly or killed? What would I do? I can't face the loss of another husband. Not to mention having nine children to raise on my own. I can't do it. Please, tell me you won't do something so dangerous again."

Clay hugged her to him tightly. He understood her concern. She'd barely been able to keep up with all her responsibilities before he came. Now they would be even more massive if he were gone. He was torn between his need to obey God when He sent the Callings and his love for Millie.

The realization that he loved Millie caught Clay by surprise. It was something he'd have to think about later. Right now he had to reassure her.

"If God calls me to do something for Him, I will. I believe He brought us together and nothing is going to tear us apart. God is faithful, and He'll keep me safe no matter what He has me do for Him."

Millie laid her head on his chest. "I hope you are right. I can't lose you."

Clay prayed that what he'd just told her was true. That God would keep him safe whenever He sent a Calling.

CHAPTER TEN

THE DAY WAS HOT AND sunny. Clay opened the door hoping to let some air through. He began sweeping the boardwalk.

"Well, isn't this just the picture of an industrious merchant." Although phrased as a question the intonation was a derisive statement.

"Good day, Mr. Terhall." Clay just managed to keep his tone neutral. "Are you needing something from the store today?"

"Not today. I'm just out for a stroll." Terhall swung his cane around nearly knocking over a display of cherries. He walked past Clay then turned around.

"I saw you out with your family on Wednesday. A fine lot of children you have there."

"Yes, they are. Thank you."

"You be sure to keep them safe. It wouldn't do for something to happen to any of them." Terhall turned and started walking back up the street.

Clay clenched his teeth. The man had just threatened his children. That was a declaration of war in Clay's mind. At the moment nothing could be done. Terhall hadn't specifically threatened anything. He'd just mentioned to keep them safe. It was the tone and obvious intent of the words.

The man was dangerous and evil. There had been a fire last week at a house near the edge of town. The woman who lived there wouldn't pay Terhall's protection 'fee.' She made it out safely but her house was destroyed. She'd moved into one of the abandoned houses. Clay and Millie gave her items she needed to start housekeeping over again.

Clay wanted to tell Marshal Sewell about the threat but he knew there was nothing that could be done until something actually occurred at the store or to some member of his family. He'd make sure nothing happened to any of them. Clay prayed for God's protective covering while he swept the boardwalk.

With no customers and everything pretty well caught up, Clay had sent the boys off to play or explore. It was Monday so Millie was upstairs doing laundry. He wanted to get the bathing room started so she'd have a laundry room, but that was going to have to wait. The boys' room still needed to be finished.

Clay was impressed with Sherman Messer's accommodations for hanging laundry. There was a staircase leading up to the roof. Drying lines were strung from poles set along the edge of the roof. With no yard it gave Millie a place to hang the laundry.

Grabbing a chair, Clay sat outside watching the few people traveling past. He knew Millie was upset about his involvement in stopping the bank robbery. He understood her concerns but he also knew that nothing would happen to him when he answered the Callings.

Millie couldn't know that. She didn't know about them.

Clay pushed back onto two legs of the chair, leaning it against the wall. Millie was more than he'd imagined when he answered her letter. She was much prettier and had such a sweet disposition. Even when she'd been so stressed from all the events that brought him to Silverpines, Millie didn't complain and wasn't snapping at the children or him. She had her moments of frustration. Having nine children would do that to anyone, but he'd see her look toward the ceiling and take a breath before dealing with whatever the issue was. When Clay asked her about it Millie smiled.

"I'm sending up a quick prayer that I don't kill any of them. So far God has been faithful and kept me from becoming a murderer. I just pray He continues to."

Clay had laughed and hugged her.

Thinking of Millie, he thought about his realization of the other day. Clay was in love with Millie. It surprised him. They'd only been together about a month. How could it happen so quickly, especially when he was still mourning Lucy?

Lucy, he'd known since they were children. They simply grew into love. No one was surprised when they announced their engagement. When she died it seemed that half of his soul died with her.

The feelings he had for Millie were new and intense. They'd come quickly as he got to know her. On the heels of that came desire. He wanted her as a husband wants his wife. Lying next to her at night was exquisite torture. Especially when she turned to face him in her sleep and her hand reached out as she slept to touch his arm or chest. It was all he could do not to pull her to him and act on his yearning.

Again, Clay went to the Lord. This time he asked that his wife would be attracted to him as he was to her. The years could stretch long and lonely if she wasn't.

Millie picked up another small skirt and pinned it to the line. At least this was the last load. Of course the first load was now ready to be taken down, sprinkled, and rolled to be ready for ironing tomorrow. She now had double the amount of laundry to do each week than she'd had before.

It took all of Monday to do the laundry and all day Tuesday to iron. Maybe if the mercantile's income was stable they could hire someone to help with it. She would start teaching Fern to iron soon. Millie didn't want to yet since her daughter had spent so much time recently taking care of the younger children. It could wait until fall or winter.

Pulling a pair of Nate's trousers from the basket she noticed they were frayed around the hem and the knees had been mended. They were hand-me-downs from Ryder. He'd need new ones to start school in. Nate was nearly as tall as Ryder now. They both had more growth to go but there wouldn't be as many hand-me-downs going forward.

Ryder looked more like his father with his blonde hair and deep blue eyes. Nate was blue-eyed but his hair was darker, a light brown Clay said was from Lucy.

Clay's eyes could mesmerize Millie. They were expressive and she saw love for all the children shining in them. Both his and hers. She was thankful neither of them showed partiality between the families. Clay had told her shortly after they married that he saw Fern, Reuben, Opal, and Abe as his own. Just as there is no partiality in God's eyes, he was not going to allow any in his. Millie agreed and took pains to treat everyone as evenly as possible.

That was one of the things she admired about Clay. Totally devoted to God, he made time every morning to read his Bible and pray. She knew he prayed also whenever he could or felt the need during the day. It was something she wanted to cultivate within herself. She tended to get lazy in her reading and time devoted strictly to prayer.

The new minister in town, Pastor James, had helped her with that. "You don't have to be doing nothing at the same time as you pray. It's good to set time aside strictly for prayer but you can pray anytime. You don't have to bow your head and fold your hands. Some of the most effective prayers are those when you are needing to lean on the Lord right then."

That opened Millie up to pray at any time no matter what she was doing. With nine children the prayers went up often as requests as well as praises.

A shirt of Clay's lay on the top in the basket now. She picked it up and laid it against her cheek. He filled it out well. It embarrassed her but she covertly watched as he dressed and undressed. His well-defined muscles rippled when he moved. She would fist her hands to keep from reaching out to him.

Pinning the shirt on the line, Millie pulled her eyebrows together, thinking. He'd told her he had an inkling that there was going to be a robbery at the bank. That wasn't a very good reason in her opinion. Then he'd implied that God had directed him to go to the marshal's office. Millie didn't know if that was true or just him giving excuses.

Scripture came to mind. The verses Clay told her were his life verses. Proverbs 3:5-6 *Trust in the Lord with all your heart and lean not on your own understanding. In all your ways acknowledge him, And He will direct your paths.*

She was going to trust and acknowledge that God was directing Clay's and her paths. If he said the Lord led him to the marshal's office, she was going to trust. Clay had said he would obey whenever God instructed him to do something. Millie might not understand it, how he knew it was God, but it wasn't necessary for her to. Just as with him, she was going to trust and lean.

That was what she'd done when she wrote the letter to Mrs. Tandy about finding a Mail Order Husband. It had brought her Clay and a passel of children to love. And love them she did. Each and every one. Even Clay.

Millie dropped the clothespin she was trying to attach to the line. She loved Clay. She had acknowledged her attraction to him, but love him? That came as a shock. All the doubts she'd had when the Cutler family stepped off the train had slowly been dispelled as the days and weeks progressed.

The way he treated her children as well as his own demonstrated his character. His hard work in the store and building the bedrooms gave her security. The plans for more adjustments to the apartment showed this thoughtfulness. Each one either helped the children or helped her.

He wasn't perfect. A typical man, Clay left clothing on the floor of the bedroom and didn't always listen when she spoke. The newspaper was always left on the floor next to the chair he favored in the parlor.

The tears that came into his eyes while Abe's head was being stitched melted her heart. Maybe that was when she started to love him. Each day it grew stronger.

What did he feel for her? Millie thought he liked her. He was a man so he was probably attracted to her physically. He often touched her gently. Sometimes he would touch her cheek and look into her eyes. She'd wake in the night with his arm around her waist. In the morning he would be on the other side of the bed.

Could he love her? She didn't know.

CHAPTER ELEVEN

GRACE WAS SITTING ON THE boardwalk on the side of the mercantile. Alone. She and Opal had an argument that ended up in a slapping match. Both thought Jackson Hershell was cute. Each girl wanted him to like her the best. As a result they couldn't play together until after supper. Ida didn't want to play with her either. She was playing with Opal.

Grace was mad at Mama too since she's the one who scolded them. It wasn't fair that Ida and Opal got to play together and she was all alone. She stuck her bottom lip out in a pout.

On top of all that there wasn't anything to look at through her magnifying glass on the boardwalk. Only ants. She'd seen those plenty of times. And you couldn't turn them over to see their legs wobble. They seemed to always get smashed when she tried.

"Well, aren't you a pretty little thing?"

Grace looked up at a man standing next to her. He was very thin with eyes that looked sunken in his face. He had a black mustache on his ashen skin.

"What do you have there?" He tapped her glass with

his cane.

"It's a magnifying glass. You make things look bigger with it." Grace held it up so he could see.

"Very nice. What do you like to look at with it?"

"Bugs. But there aren't any here. Just ants."

"I know something you can look at." The man smiled.

"What?"

"Crumple up some paper, maybe an old newspaper. Then hold your glass so the sunlight shines through it. Wait and something magical happens."

"What?"

The man smiled. "You'll have to try it to find out." He moved past and left Grace alone.

Something magical? Grace's eyes lit up with excitement. She knew where she could get a newspaper. Pa always left his on the floor by his chair. She ran around and up the stairs going into the apartment. No one was there. She grabbed the newspaper and ran back to where she'd been sitting before.

Crumpling up several pages, she mounded them together. Squatting beside them she held her magnifying glass so the sunlight focused on the paper. Nothing happened. Then she remembered the man said she had to wait.

Grace made the bright spot on the paper very small. It began to smoke, then the paper began to burn. Flames licked the paper growing bigger.

Grace jumped up and backed away. Turning she ran to the front of the store. Pa was sitting in a chair leaned back against the wall.

"Pa, fire, fire. I made fire," she screamed.

The chair legs banged down on the wood. "What?

Where?"

Grace ran to where the fire was scorching the boardwalk. Pa followed. He stamped the fire out. It seemed to take a lot of stamping. She stood with her back to the wall, her hands pressed against her mouth.

Finally, the fire was out. The boards were black charred wood. Pa turned to her. Grace ran to him and was enveloped in a huge hug.

"Are you okay? Did you get burned?" Pa asked.

Grace was crying. "No."

Pa carried her around to the chair he'd been sitting on. They sat with her in his lap. When Grace stopped crying he held his handkerchief to her nose for her to blow.

"How did you start that?"

"A man told me there'd be magic if I focused the sunlight on crumpled newspaper. He didn't say it would start a fire." Tears slid down her face again.

"What did the man look like?" Pa was frowning.

"Skinny with a mustache. His eyes looked sunk in his face."

Pa's frown got deeper. "Grace, he's not a nice man. If he tries to talk to you again, you or your sisters, walk away. Come home. Don't talk to him. What he told you to do was dangerous."

"But I didn't know it was."

Pa hugged her to him. "I know. You see why he's not a nice man? He wanted you to do something that could have hurt you."

Grace nodded.

"Let's go find your mama. Maybe you can help her with the laundry. She might let you sprinkle the clothes."

* * *

Grace was happily sprinkling clothing when Clay pulled Millie out of the kitchen. Leading her by the hand, they went to their bedroom.

"Terhall told Grace she could do magic with her magnifying glass. She started a fire."

"What?" Millie turned to go back to Grace. Clay stopped her with a hand on her arm.

"She wasn't hurt. She came and got me. I was able to stomp it out. She was scared more than anything."

"What are we going to do? The man wants money and will do anything to the people who won't pay." Millie's frantic expression tugged at his heart.

"First, we'll talk to the children and tell them about him. Warn them. Tomorrow, I'm going to talk with Marshal Sewell. Tell him about the threats and what happened today. I'm not sure what he can do, but at least he'll be aware. Maybe they'll step up the watch around the store."

"What good will that do?"

"Maybe warn him away. Maybe we or they can catch him trying something."

Millie laid her head against his chest. "Can't we just shoot him?"

Clay chuckled. "I know how you feel, but no. The best thing we can do is pray for God to keep us all safe and for Terhall to come to justice."

CHAPTER TWELVE

NATE CLOSED THE BOOK. IT had been raining the last couple of days so he'd spent the time after his chores reading. Tom Sawyer and Huckleberry Finn had such interesting and fun adventures. He'd just finished reading both books.

Today, the sun was out and it was getting hot. Just the type of day Tom and Huck would spend on the river. Maybe even on an island. Nate dropped the book and went to find Ryder.

"Hey, didn't Jackson say there was an island in the river?" he asked his older brother.

"Yeah. Why?" Ryder asked. He was whittling. Or at least he was attempting to. So far all he'd done was make a pile of shavings on the floor.

"We could go there and pretend to be Tom Sawyer and Huck Finn."

"How are we going to get there?" Another shaving fell.

"By boat, silly. We'd row over." Nate wondered why Ryder was so dense.

"What boat?"

"Didn't Jackson say he had a boat he'd found after the earthquake? We can ask him to go along. It'll be fun. We can fish and he knows how to clean and cook them. We can hunt some rabbits. There may be berries and wild onion on the island."

Ryder was catching Nate's enthusiasm. "Yeah. We've gone hunting with Pa. We can set a rabbit snare. Skin 'em and roast them over a fire."

Nate laughed. "Yeah. Do you suppose Grace would let us take her magnifying glass?"

They knew about Grace's fire. Pa had warned them all about Mr. Terhall and what to do if he came around. Don't talk to him. Go find Pa.

Ryder laughed. "I'll go find Jackson. I don't think he has any jobs today. I'm sure he'll want to go."

"I'll see if Mama has any food we can take. Just in case." Nate headed out of the room.

"Don't tell her where we're going. She might not want us on the river," Ryder instructed as he headed down the stairs into the back room of the store.

"Right."

Soon, there were three boys rowing across the river to an island just east of town. Nate had skirted around the issue of where they were going just saying that Jackson was going to show them around outside of town. Nothing about the river was mentioned.

They had knives, a hatchet, the bundle with sandwiches, fruit, and cookies inside. Their fishing poles were in the bottom of the boat along with a small metal kit of tackle. They had string for snares, and in each boy's back pocket was a slingshot.

Rowing to the far end of the island, they beached the

rowboat and tied the line to a fallen tree hanging out over the water. The side of the island was scarred from the mudslide. There were logs that had washed ashore scattered along.

"This sure looks different from the last time I was here," Jackson said. "That was last year. One of the loggers brought me over. We fished and found a passel of blueberry bushes. They were this big." He held his thumb and forefinger in a circle.

"Let's go explore. Then we can fish," Ryder said. "I'm gonna be Daniel Boone." He strutted up the beach.

"I'm Davy Crockett," yelled Jackson, following.

Nate frowned. Tom Sawyer didn't sound nearly as exciting as Boone or Crocket. Inspiration struck. "I'm Nugget Nate Ryder." He ran after the older boys.

The blueberry bushes were where Jackson had remembered them. The berries were as large too. When the three friends were finished shoving them in their mouths all the hands and faces were stained blue.

"Maybe we should play cowboys and Indians. We have war paint on," Ryder suggested.

"Nah. Who's going to want to be the Indians. They always lose and end up dead." Nate jumped up and swung his hand at a tree branch.

"Let's fish. I know a place where they're always biting," Jackson said. "It's on the far side of the island from town. No one will see us."

"Good idea. Let's go." Nate and Ryder followed Jackson as he snuck through the woods. Each pretending to be the legendary hero they'd chosen.

* * *

Clay locked the door to the store. The uneasy feeling of a pending Calling had been nagging at him all afternoon. He wondered if it really was a Calling or simply a father worried about his sons off scouting the area with a friend. They'd gone before lunch.

Ben and Reuben were put out that they hadn't been asked to go along. They'd spent part of the afternoon in the back room until Clay got tired of hearing their grumbling. He sympathized with Moses who had a million Israelites grumbling as they wandered the wilderness. Ben and Reuben were sent to the park.

Clay went in search of Millie when he reached the apartment. The girls were all in their bedroom playing with Kitty. The poor thing was wearing a doll's bonnet.

Abe was playing with alphabet blocks in the parlor by the kitchen door. Clay smiled as the toddler built a tower then knocked it down.

"Something smells good." Clay came up behind Millie who was at the stove stirring a pot of something brown. He slipped his arm around her waist and leaned over to see and sniff.

"Shepherd's Pie. I'm making chocolate pudding for dessert."

"Have the boys come back yet?"

"Not yet." Millie swiped at his hand when he reached for a biscuit from the pan on a warming shelf. He was successful in taking one and took a bite. Soft, fluffy, warm, and delicious.

"It's early. With the days so long it might be a while. I can remember going hunting with my brothers or friends and not coming back until it was almost dark." Clay tried to shake the uneasy feeling crawling over his back.

"I suppose," Millie said. "They had food with them and I know they took their fishing poles."

Abe came in and pointed to the window. "Rainin'."

They hadn't noticed since it was a gentle rain not making any sound.

"That'll bring them home," Clay said. "But let's not wait supper on them. They may be a while and the children must be hungry."

"The children, huh?" Millie smiled then handed him a basket filled with biscuits and indicated he should take them into the dining room.

By the time supper was over and the dishes done Clay's back was crawling. It was a Calling and it was about the boys. He could tell Millie was worried too.

Clay did what he always did when the Calling wasn't clear. He prayed. Sitting in his favorite parlor chair, he ignored the newspaper and closed his eyes.

Lord, I know you have us all in the palm of your hand. I thank you for that. Nothing can take us from it. I'm listening to Your Calling about my boys. You know where they are and are wanting me to go find them. I can't do that unless You show me where they are. Please, Lord.

In his mind an image of a spot along the river appeared. He knew it was where the boys liked to fish. Then another place along the river appeared. He'd never seen it before but that didn't matter. Clay knew the Calling would lead him to them. Getting up, he went to get his Mackintosh and Stetson.

Millie was reading to the children in the girls' room.

"I'm going to get the boys. I know where they are."

"You do? How?"

"I'll explain later. I need to get them now." He left, but before he exited the building he strapped on his gun belt.

"Rats," Ryder said. "It's starting to rain. We won't be able to cook the fish now." They'd caught several nice bass and filleted them.

"Let's head back to the boat. We can cook them at home, if Mama lets us." Nate wiped his knife off on his trousers.

They found some large leaves and wrapped the fish inside and gathered the gear. As they walked they checked the snares but found no rabbits caught in them.

"I don't think there's many rabbits on the island. I've never caught any," Jackson said. "Only fish. There may be coons here though."

When they arrived at the beach the boat was gone. Only the end of the rope used to tie it remained. It had been cut with a sharp blade.

Ryder and Nate looked at each other. "Terhall," they said at the same time.

"What?" Jackson asked.

"We think Terhall or his henchman cut the rope to strand us here," Ryder said. "He wants Pa and Mama to pay him money for protection. He's sort of threatened. Not come right out and said it, but the message was pretty clear."

"He tricked Grace into starting a fire with her magnifying glass. It scared her real bad." Nate untied the rope.

"Let's head to the other end of the island. That's where Pa will find us." Ryder started walking along the beach.

"How will he know?" Jackson asked.

Ryder and Nate exchanged looks. Pa had warned them not to talk about the Callings.

"It's the closest place to town. Makes sense to go there. Maybe they'll be able to see us from town." Ryder knew that wasn't the reason. He knew they'd be found. There was that sensation he was learning was how he felt the Calling. This time it was for them to be rescued from the island. He figured Nate knew he'd had one.

As they walked the length of the island the rain came down harder, soaking them to the skin.

Clay's first stop was the marshal's office. It was Marshal Sewell's evening to be on duty so he greeted Clay when he entered.

"Evening, Clay. What can I do for you?"

"My boys, as well as Jackson Hershell, went out today but haven't come back. I'm sure Terhall has something to do with it."

"Why do you think that?"

"He's made threatening remarks. Nothing that could be evidence. That we had a nice family of children and we should be careful. That we wouldn't want any of them to be hurt.

"He tricked Grace into starting a fire on the boardwalk with her magnifying glass. Now the boys are gone. They said they were going to explore outside of town with Jackson Hershell. None of them came home when it started to rain."

"Sounds suspicious. Shall I get up a search party?"

"I don't think we need one. I know where to start looking. I've had a Calling. It's not complete. I don't know for sure where they are, but we need to start at that fishing spot they like to go to."

Sewell got up, put on his raincoat and Stetson, grabbed his rifle, and followed Clay out into the rain.

Jackson led the way. At times they had to leave the beach because of logs or that the beach simply wasn't there. The days of rain made their boots become heavy with mud and sand. Tree branches caught on their fishing poles and thorns grabbed at their clothing.

"It seems as if everything is trying to slow us down," complained Nate. "I sure hope Pa is there when we get to the end of the island."

"He will be." Ryder stopped. "Jackson, stop," he yelled. When the teen didn't, Ryder dropped his pole and ran to him, grabbing him by the arm. "Stop."

"What? Why? I'm cold and it's raining harder."

"Just wait. We have to wait." Ryder looked at Nate who'd caught up with them. "I just know. Something's going to happen."

They waited a moment. Jackson opened his mouth to say something when a loud cracking was heard. Just ahead where they would have been walking a tree fell, crashing to the ground.

Jackson looked at Ryder, his eyes wide with shock.

"How did you know that tree was going to fall?"

"I didn't. I just knew we had to stop and wait." Ryder exchanged a glance with Nate.

"But how? Did you hear something? I didn't." Jackson looked from brother to brother.

"When you're listening to God, sometimes He gives a warning. I've been praying that we get home safely. Thanking God that He's going to get us home. I just knew He was telling me to stop and wait. Nothing else. I didn't know the tree was going to fall. Just that we were supposed to stop."

Nate nodded slightly, letting Ryder know his explanation was good.

Jackson looked from Ryder to the tree they now had to climb over or go around and back at his friends. "Is it safe to go on now?"

"Yeah, let's go." Ryder took his pole from Nate who'd picked it up.

The tree was a large one, the trunk too wide to climb over. It extended clear into the river so they had to move further inland to move past it.

Jackson kept glancing at Ryder, questions in his eyes.

"That's the boat Jackson Hershell uses. He'd go out with one of the loggers and they'd fish or hunt. The logger died in the mudslide." Sewell stepped into the water and grabbed the side, pulling the rowboat to shore. It had floated into the inlet many townsfolk used for fishing.

Clay knew it wasn't there by accident. He helped

beach it and picked up the rope trailing from the bow. "This has been cut. See, the end's straight instead of ragged as if it was worn through."

"Yep." Sewell looked across the river. "They must be upstream. It had to float down here. Did they tell anyone where they were going?"

'No, I think they didn't want anyone to know they were going onto the river."

"There's a large island upriver a ways. We'll head there first." Sewell lifted his leg and climbed into the boat. Clay followed.

"That's where they'll be. At the near end."

Sewell looked at him as he pushed off with an oar. "You know that?"

"Yeah. I had a Calling to come here. Now I see the end of an island."

"Well, I'm not one to question a Calling." Sewell bent to the oars moving the boat upstream.

Clay picked up a tin can and began bailing the water collecting in the boat from the rain.

"There's the island," Clay said after a while.

Sewell turned around on his seat and adjusted the angle he was rowing to aim the boat toward the island's point. "Can you see them?"

"No, not yet. Let's land and scout around."

Clay jumped out to drag the craft onto the shore when they arrived. He didn't see anyone. *Come on, Lord. You Called me here.*

Clay moved inland just into the woods from the beach. "Ryder, Nate, Jackson," he hollered. He bent his head to listen. He yelled again. Sewell turned to go in a different direction

"Pa."

Clay moved forward. It was Ryder's voice. Then he heard Nate yell too. He moved faster. Sewell came alongside. They shoved through thickets, hearing the boys doing the same.

Two bodies slammed into his. Clay wrapped his arms around them. "You're safe. We're here."

Jackson was being hugged by Sewell. Once the joy of finding each other was over they stepped back.

"The rope on the boat was cut," Nate said. He fished the piece he had out of his pocket. "See."

"We know. We found the boat in the fishing cove by town." Sewell took the rope, looking at it.

"I knew you'd be coming for us. We headed to this end of the island. We were at the other end," Ryder said.

"Good thinking." Clay patted his son's shoulder.

"Ryder made us stop. Then a tree fell right where we were going. He knew something was going to happen." Jackson told Sewell.

"God just told me to stop. So we did."

"Always a wise thing to obey the Lord," Sewell said.

"Well, let's get in the boat and back to town. I'm wet and cold and your Mama is most likely frantic with worry." Clay gave Nate a light shove toward the shore. When Nate grinned at him Clay frowned. "We'll be having a chat about telling us where you're going when we get home."

Millie met them at the door. She didn't care that they were wet. She hugged each one tightly to her, kissing their heads and thanking the Lord that they were home and healthy.

"I was so worried. Where were you?" She gave Ryder a little shake.

"They had gone to an island upriver." Clay rolled up his raincoat so it wouldn't drip on the rug.

"What?" Millie frowned at both boys. Hands on her hips, she said, "There's hot water for baths on the stove. You get warm and dry, then I'll fix your supper."

"Can you fry up our catch? We even cleaned them." Nate held up the pouch and pulled out the crumpled, leaf wrapped bundle of fish. Clay smacked him lightly on the back of the head.

CHAPTER THIRTEEN

MILLIE WATCHED CLAY AS HE changed into his nightshirt. She was thankful the boys were okay and home. Now she had some questions. This was the second time Clay 'knew' something was going on without any reason he should. First, it was the bank robbery. Now, he'd known where the boys were before he even left the building. She frowned when Clay dropped his socks on the floor but didn't say anything.

When he got into bed, Millie rolled on her side to look at him. "Okay, mister. How did you know where they were? We had no clue they'd taken a boat to the island. While you think of an answer to that, figure out how to tell me you knew about the bank going to be robbed."

Clay lay on his back staring at the ceiling. "I've delayed in telling you because it can sound crazy. People in Stones Creek know all about them. I haven't said anything because some people don't or won't understand."

"Understand what?"

Clay took a deep breath and turned on his side. "Don't say anything until I'm done. It's a complicated story.

"People in my family have Callings. They are from the Lord and always help save people, bring outlaws to justice, that sort of thing. It goes back in my family a long way. My Grandma Aggie, as she put it, gathered girls in need to her. She'd come across young girls or teens who were in desperate situations and either take them in or help them in whatever way she could. She just knew when one needed her. She'd know where they were and find them.

"My pa didn't have the Callings too much or he never mentioned having any, but then, Stones Creek had my great-uncle coming to town whenever there was a real problem. My great-uncle was Nugget Nate Ryder."

Millie started to say something but Clay placed his fingers on her lip.

"Nugget Nate had the strongest Callings of anyone. He went all over the country following the Lord to where he and his skills were needed. His grandson, Nathan Ryder, is my second cousin. He's known as The Preacher.

"Nathan came to Stones Creek one summer with Nate and Aunt Penny. He taught me a lot about hunting and shooting and living off the land. He helped me understand the Callings, how to recognize them and figure them out.

"I had a Calling that day of the bank robbery. I wasn't sure until I headed to the jail what was going to happen, but by the time I got there it was clear in my head. Marshal Sewell grew up in Kentucky on the mountain where Nate and my grandma were born and raised. He knows about the Callings.

"Today, I had one about the boys. I knew where to go to be able to find them. First, to the fishing spot where we found the boat. Then, to the island." Clay stopped, waiting for her response.

Millie looked at him. "You should have told me before now. I'm your wife. You should have trusted me."

Clay brushed her cheek with the back of his fingers. "I didn't want you to think I was off in the head."

"I know all about Nugget Nate and his Callings. I read all the books with his stories in them when I was growing up. They were wonderful stories. I loved them."

"They were even better when he told them." Clay chuckled. "I, and every boy he ever met, have the very knife Jim Bowie gave him after he killed some man. I can't remember the rest of it. Nathan said he gave them out every time they stopped."

Millie laughed. "I'll bet you and every other boy thought that was the greatest thing ever."

"We did," Clay said, then he sobered. "Ryder's having Callings. He had one today which saved their lives. He was Called to stop and wait. He made the other boys stop. A huge tree fell just where they would have been if they hadn't stopped. He had a small one about Terhall a while back. Knew the man wasn't a good man. We've talked about it. Nate knows about them, but I don't think he's had any. He's a little young yet. Comes on about Ryder's age."

Millie nodded, thinking. "Ryder, Nate, Ben, you named your sons after Nugget Nate and your father."

"Yes, my pa, Nate, and Nathan were a great influence on me as I grew up. It was a way I could honor their legacy."

Clay lay against Millie's back, his arm around her waist. She was sleeping. He never got in this position until she was asleep. He wasn't going to pressure her, but waiting to make her his wife in more than name was getting harder.

She'd surprised him with her easy acceptance of the Callings. He'd never thought she'd know anything about Nugget Nate or The Preacher. He should have known. Nugget Nate was a legend. They even had some of the books for sale in the store.

Maybe he should tell her of his attraction. Maybe even of his love. What if she wasn't attracted to him? What if she didn't want him? She seemed to enjoy when he gave her small touches. Sometimes she'd lean against him.

Millie seemed to love his children. She'd been in tears greeting Ryder and Nate when they got home. Her actions toward them were definitely that of a mother worried over her offspring. Clay grinned in the dark. She'd even fried the pieces of fish they'd brought home, broken and battered as they were.

Millie turned in his arms until she was facing him. Her eyes were open. "Are you ever going to hold me when we are awake or only when you think I'm asleep?"

Clay looked at the invitation in her eyes. He drew her closer and pressed his lips to hers.

CHAPTER FOURTEEN

AS A PUNISHMENT FOR NOT telling anyone where they were going, or asking permission, Ryder and Nate were working on the bedrooms again. They were nailing lath to the framing and would be plastering as soon as that was done. Until the room was completed they weren't allowed any free time. This encouraged diligence on the part of the young men.

Clay was inspecting the day's accomplishment. "You're making good progress. Just the ceiling left to lath. Another day or so and you'll be able to start plastering."

The boys looked up at the vast space and sighed. "Yes, sir."

Clay chuckled and rubbed each boy on the head. "Come on. Let's go wash up. It's just about time for supper."

As they preceded him out the door Clay stopped. A frisson went up his back. Something was going to happen. He wasn't sure what but knew the Calling was something dealing with his family.

Neither Terhall nor his henchmen had been seen in

town lately. The marshal checked in with Clay several times a week. No one thought he'd left Silverpines for good.

Clay didn't say anything about his Calling to Millie, but he thought she realized something as he wasn't entering into the conversations going on around the table. After supper he went down to the mercantile checking that the doors and windows were locked. He checked that all the stoves were cold and the lanterns out.

"Is everything all right?" Millie asked when he came back upstairs.

"Yes. I just went to check on things." Clay picked up Abe who was pulling on his pant leg. "You want to play a bit, buddy."

"Horsie," said Abe.

Clay got down on his knees and let Abe crawl on his back. As he gently bucked the toddler up and down, Clay prayed for God's protection and for him to know what to do when the Calling revealed itself.

Clay rolled over, turning away from Millie. He'd been holding her as they slept. He stared into the darkness. A vision of flames burst into his mind. Sitting up he patted Millie on the back. "Get up. We need to get the children out of here."

"What?" Millie's voice was groggy with sleep.

Clay was pulling his britches on. "It's a Calling. There's going to be a fire. We need to get the children."

Millie jumped out of bed and grabbed a dressing gown, slipping it on over her nightgown. Clay had his boots on and grabbed the gun belt he kept beside the bed at night.

A knock sounded on their door. Ryder opened it, coming in before Clay could answer. "Pa, something's wrong. I just know it."

"I know. Get your brothers and wake Fern. We need to get out as soon as we can. Then you head to the marshal's office. There's going to be a fire."

Ryder turned and ran from the room.

"I'll get Abe. You get the girls. Head to the park. Make sure all the boys and girls but Ryder are with you." Clay ran into Abe's room scooping him up from his crib.

Millie was waking Opal and Grace. She picked up Ida. "Come girls. We need to get out now."

"Where's Kitty?" Opal cried.

Fern ran into the room. "What's going on? Is it another earthquake. Ryder said we had to leave."

"An earthquake?" Grace squealed. She was clutching the doll Lucy had given her for Christmas. Her eyes were wide with fear.

"We need to get out, Fern. Don't ask questions now. Find Kitty." Millie was grabbing blankets from the beds.

"Come on, girls," Clay yelled.

"Here's Kitty." Fern pulled the kitten out from under Ida's bed. "Come on Opal. I have her."

Clay turned and went into the hall. Nate, Ben, and Reuben were heading for the parlor. "Nate, come take Abe. Head to the park. I'll be there as soon as I can."

"Where are you going?" Nate asked.

"To stop this. Go."

Clay made sure everyone got out through the parlor door then ran down the back stairs. The door to the storeroom was ajar. Either someone was in the store or Ryder had gone not making sure the door was latched when he left. He stuck his head out the door scanning the back street behind the building. Nothing and no sound.

Pulling out his revolver, Clay moved quietly to search the store. If someone had been in there they would have heard all the footsteps from upstairs. That would have scared them off.

No one was there and there was no sign of a fire. He unlocked the front door and went outside. Clouds obscured any moonlight. He looked toward the park but couldn't see anything in the darkness. He prayed his family was safe. Also, if this was arson he'd catch whoever was trying to burn them out.

Since no alarm had been called from his family, Clay turned away from the park and moved quietly along the wall to the corner. He peeked around then pulled back quickly.

Terhall and another man were kneeling on the boardwalk. It looked like they had pried up the scorched boards from where Grace had set the fire. There were flames coming from the hole. Unless he shot one of them, there was no way he could singlehandedly apprehend both of them.

A light further down the street toward the river flashed. Then again. Clay hoped it was Ryder and whatever lawman was on duty tonight. He hated waiting, knowing that the fire was growing every second.

Stepping back so his movements wouldn't be noticed,

Clay waved his arms. Would they see him in the darkness? The lantern flashed twice. Then it went out. There was an empty lot across from the mercantile that would reveal them if they shined the light.

Clay ran around the corner, his gun in his hand. "Stop, I've got you covered. Dowse that fire."

Footsteps sounded running toward him. "You heard the man. Do it." The voice was that of Deputy Gene Autry. He had his gun trained on the men too.

"You're too late," Terhall laughed. "The wall's caught. This place will burn to the ground, your family with it."

Just then a bell started ringing. In the park was a pole with a large bell on top. It was used to call the townsfolk together to help stop fires. The last time it was used was when the woman's house burned. It had been blazing too much by the time everyone arrived.

"Lie down on the street. Both of you." Gene handcuffed them. Once that was done, Clay ran into the store getting blankets. He began beating the flames as people started coming.

Siding boards were pulled off and buckets of water were pumped, brought, and poured on the flames. Lightning flashed as rain began pouring down, aiding the efforts to dowse the flames.

Clay stepped back, panting from his efforts. Suddenly Millie was in his arms.

"Are you all right?" She hugged him as if she'd never let him go.

"Yes, we caught them red handed, Terhall and his man. They were just getting the fire started. Where are the children?"

"I left them in the bandstand. They could stay dry

there."

"I think it's out," Sewell said. He'd come to the call of the alarm bell. "We'll need to check inside though."

Millie stepped back, but Clay kept his arm around her waist. He didn't want to let her go. If he hadn't listened to his Calling he could have lost her as well as all their children.

"Pa," Ryder said, causing both he and Millie to turn around. "I saw them starting to pry the boards up so I went around the other way and behind the hotel to get to the jail. Then I went and rang the bell when Deputy Autry and you caught them."

"Good thinking." Clay patted Ryder's shoulder.

The rain was letting up and people were heading back to their homes. Millie and Clay thanked them all for helping.

"You'll need to come in tomorrow and make a statement. With them being caught in the act, it'll be a pretty open and shut case. They'll go to prison for a long time. Arson is a felony," Sewell said. He grabbed Terhall's arm and Autry took the other man's. They headed toward the jail.

Clay pulled Millie closer to him and kissed her. "You go get the children. Ryder and I will check the store. I don't want any embers to flare up."

They were finishing pulling boards down inside when everyone came in. Four little girls ran to him, crying out their fears. He knelt and hugged them to him.

"It's okay. Just some boards need to be replaced. We caught the bad men who did this."

"The man who tricked me into starting that fire?" Grace asked.

"Yes, sweetie, that man."

"Good. He's a bad man." She jabbed her hands onto her hips and frowned. "He needs to be sorry for what he did and ask God to forgive him."

"He certainly does," Millie said. "Let's go upstairs and have some cocoa. I think it will help us all get to sleep."

Clay watched Millie herd the nine children he loved so much through to the back room thanking the Lord for the Calling that saved them from disaster.

The children were nestled in their beds, calm now. It had taken a while for the fears to settle. Abe fell asleep in his highchair. Ida's head drooped onto the table. Millie and Clay took turns getting into dry clothing, not wanting to leave the children alone. Ben and Reuben wanted a blow by blow of the events. Clay had described it all, playing down the fire and emphasizing Ryder's role.

Millie settled under the covers, lying on her side waiting for Clay to climb in bed. There was a lantern turned low illuminating the room in a soft glow. He sat on the edge and rubbed his face.

"Are you okay?" she asked.

"Yes, just trying to relax. I'm still keyed up from everything." Clay lay down and faced her. "I've never had such a threat to my family before. All my Callings have been less dangerous." He chuckled. "Not at all like Nugget Nate's or The Preacher's. I'll have to write Nathan and tell him about this. And that Ryder is having Callings."

"He did tonight, didn't he? That's why he knew before we woke him." Millie scooted closer. Clay pulled her to him and she laid her head on his shoulder.

"Yes."

Millie could tell Clay wanted to say something but was hesitating. She wanted to say something to him too. That she loved him and had been scared to death he'd be hurt or killed. She waited, letting him gather his thoughts.

Clay turned on his side and stroked her cheek. "Millie, this may be too soon. You may not want to hear this, but I have to say it. I need to tell you. Millie, I love you. I have for some time. I thank God every day for the Calling that brought us here to Silverpines."

Millie blinked the sudden flooding of her eyes away.

"Don't cry, sweetheart. You don't have to say anything. You don't have to love me. I just hope you like me a little." He kissed each eye.

Millie snuggled closer and touched the stubble on his cheek. "I don't like you a little. I love you a lot. I have for a while but wasn't sure how you felt about me.

"When I placed that ad in the Grooms Gazette I only wanted a shopkeeper to help with the responsibilities of running the store and raising my children. I received much more than that." She chuckled. "Five more children to love, but the best thing is you. You're so much more than just the shopkeeper I wanted. You're the man I've come to love with all my heart."

Clay didn't say anything else. He simply brought his lips to hers, kissing her with all the love he had in his heart.

EPILOGUE

Millie tucked the last of the oranges in the nine stockings hanging from hooks on the wall next to the parlor stove. There was a pair of mittens or gloves she'd knitted in each one. Under the Christmas tree was a gift for each child chosen carefully by Clay and her. There was a wool vest she'd sewn for Clay. She had no clue what he'd gotten for her. He wouldn't let her shake the box, making Reuben put it clear in the back under the branches. The children had laughed at her antics of pouting at Clay.

This year had seen devastating losses which gave way to blessings the likes of which she'd never have imagined. The earthquakes and their ramifications had nearly destroyed her. Then Clay came with the surprise of his family. Now they were hers too. She couldn't imagine not having those five children to love.

The nine youngsters had blended into a true

family. There were some days Millie felt as if all she did was stop teasing and bickering. Having the mercantile with its continual chores was effective in providing consequences for poor behavior. Even Ida could be set wiping down the lowest shelves.

Millie took her night lantern and went into the bathing room. Clay had completed the remodeling of the apartment in the fall and Millie loved it. Being able to do laundry in the sinks he'd installed and having a real bathtub made things so much easier. She ran a brush through her hair and straightened her dressing gown.

When she finished, Millie checked Abe. He was asleep, his thumb in his mouth. Next she looked into the girls' room. She smiled. Kitty was sleeping between Grace and Opal. Fern was in bed with Ida snuggled up to her.

Fern loved her room, enjoying the privacy it gave her. Tonight though, Christmas Eve, she had chosen to stay with the little girls.

Two sets of bunkbeds sat on opposite walls of the boys' room. When Abe moved in there was room for another bed. Or maybe they would add another bedroom. She'd need to discuss it with Clay.

Turning from the sleeping boys, Millie opened the linen closet across the hall and took out a small package. It was for Clay. She hoped he understood what the gift meant. Hoped he liked it. She'd made them especially to give him. This gift she'd give him privately in their room. He'd gone to bed before she filled the stockings. The store had been busy today and there had been worship service this evening.

Going into their room, Millie saw that Clay was in bed waiting for her. She smiled. He smiled back. She didn't know if it was part of his Calling, but it seemed they could communicate with just a look.

Millie set the lantern on his bedside table then moved around the bed to her side. He'd drawn the covers back so she climbed in, lying on her side facing him. "I have a gift for you. I wanted to give it to you privately." She held the small gift out to him.

Clay turned on his side. "You didn't have to give me another gift. Whatever the present is under the tree is plenty." He took it from her hand.

"Open it." Millie bit her lip wondering if he'd like it.

Pulling the ribbon he untied the bow. The paper loosened revealing what was inside.

Clay looked at her, his eyes bright yet questioning. "Are you sure? Happy?"

Millie smiled. "Yes. I'm very happy about it."

Clay picked up the tiny white crocheted booties. "When?"

"June, I think."

Clay kissed her and Millie could feel all the love he had for her. She hoped he could tell how much she loved him as she responded to his kiss.

When they parted, Clay said, "Okay, I'll finally agree to hire someone to help with the laundry. I think with ten children you deserve to have a mother's helper."

Millie laughed and hugged him. "I'm going to hold you to that. Other than laundry, I don't think there will be much difference between nine children and ten."

Clay kissed her again. "I'm so thankful you wanted a shopkeeper, and I'm so glad you chose me."

What's Next in Silverpines

Want to find out what happens next in Silverpines? Follow the link below for a Sneak Peek of *Wanted: Preacher*.

Book four in the Silverpines's series by Renae Westlyn.

Sneak Peek

georgemcvey.weebly.com/silverpines-preview.html

A note from Sophie

I hope you enjoyed **Wanted: Shopkeeper**. Please take a moment to leave a review on Amazon. For independently publishing authors like myself, the reviews are extremely valuable in getting our work noticed. If you take just a few minutes you could help someone else find their next favorite book.

If you'd like to be notified of upcoming releases please sign up for my newsletter. It only comes to you when there is actual real, news about my books. You need not worry that your information will ever be released to anyone in any way for anything. I hate spam as much as you do.

http://www.sophie-dawson.com/subscription.html

Thank you.

Sophie

* * *

Want to read more of my books? Head to my Amazon page:

https://www.amazon.com/Sophie-Dawson/e/B0084POHB6/

Sophie Dawson is an award-winning author of Christian fiction romance both historical and contemporary. An eclectic conglomeration of interests and accomplishments, she has made up stories in her head all her life. Now she types them out. Her critically acclaimed series include Cottonwood, Stones Creek, and Love's Infestation. She's also been part of several Multi-Author projects.

Made in the USA
Columbia, SC
29 March 2019